The [...]
Wit[...]

By [...] Miller

The Legend of the Witch Wolves

Copyright © Andrew John Miller 2017

All rights reserved. No reproduction, copy or transmission of this publication in any form to be made without express written permission.

ISBN - 978 0 9957926 0 9

Published by Deep Dark Forest 2017

www.deepdarkforest.net

Cornwall - 1760

Chapter 1.

She is shivering, but it is not from the cold. Her heart is thumping and her guts have tied themselves in knots. She feels as if she will be sick if she has to wait a moment longer.

The waiting is the hardest part.

It is not too late to change her mind. She could turn the horse around and go home. No one would ever know. It would be the sensible thing to do.

When was the last time she did the sensible thing?

The stallion stamps impatiently, his whole body trembling with pent up energy. She leans forward in the saddle and whispers into his ear.

"It won't be long. And when I'm done I shall need you to run like the wind!"

The horse gives a bad tempered snort and lowers his head.

She rests her face against the stallion's neck. She closes her eyes and breathes in the dark musk of horse sweat. She feels the warmth of him against her cheek. Her heart slows and the tide of her terror draws back.

The stallion is jet black, with a single blaze of white on his nose in the shape of a knife blade. Steam rises from his flanks, mixing with the night mist, gathering about horse and black clad rider in a haze that makes them all but invisible where they wait in the shadow of the ruined house.

The land is so deep in fog that the hilltop might be an island, adrift on a moonlit ocean. At the top of the hill stands the gibbet, looming over the world like an omen of doom. A man-sized iron cage hung from a tall wooden post, the gibbet is where the mortal remains of criminals are displayed after they have been hung on the gallows. The gibbet has played host to murderers, pickpockets, pirates and highwaymen, it has held poor men who stole bread for their starving children and innocent men who did nothing worse than displease the Magistrate. Innocent or guilty, they all went the same way; picked clean by the ravens and fallen to bones upon the earth of Reaver's Hill.

The gibbet turns slowly on its chain, the rusty iron grating harshly in the stillness of the night. The bars seem to hold the moon prisoner, the mouth in the bone white face drawn open in a silent howl. If things go badly tonight then it will be her bones in the gibbet cage at the next full moon.

She turns away with a shudder.

The stallion lifts his head, ears twitching. Then comes the sound that she has been waiting for; the thunder of hooves and the rattle of carriage wheels on the road below.
"Now!" she hisses, kicking the stallion forward.

* * * * *

The coachman sees the fallen tree only just in time to halt the carriage. He stands up in his seat, reins back the horses and the coach skids to a halt, dumping the passenger in the back onto the floor with a thump. Mr Periwigge clambers painfully to his feet and picks up his hat. He pulls down the window, leans out and yells up at the driver:
"You almost killed me - you idiot! What the blazes is going on!"
"See for yourself," replies Noah."The road's blocked."
Mr Periwigge peers ahead into the fog. The remains of a dead tree have fallen down onto the road, leaving a gaping hole in the steep bank above.
"It's only an old stump," snarls Mr Periwigge. "Get out and shift it or I'll have you horsewhipped!"
Mr Periwigge is in a foul temper. The journey from Bristol has taken two days and it has rained most of the way. He is battered and bruised and the thought of his final destination makes him shudder. Colby Hall is a godforsaken place at the best of times, half ruined and dreadfully damp. The wind howls constantly in the chimneys and the fires are forever going out. There are rumours that the hall is haunted - something that Mr Periwigge has no trouble in believing.

  Mr Periwigge tries to tell himself that it is money alone that makes him do Squire Colby's bidding but he knows in his heart it is not. There is a great deal of money to be made in his business with Josia Colby but it is fear that makes Mr Periwigge come running whenever he is called - fear of what the Squire might do to him if he refuses.

Muttering curses at the verminous Mr Periwigge, the coachman is making ready to hand the reins to the coach guard when the guard gives a gasp and grabs him by the arm.

"Noah - Look out!"

A dark rider looms out of the mist. A rider wrapped in a heavy cloak and mounted on a tall, black horse.

The stallion comes alongside the carriage, bringing the rider level with the men on the driving seat. The rider glares at them from under the brim of the hat and they feel the heat of the stallion's breath on their faces.

"Stand down lads!" calls the masked rider, drawing a pistol and levelling it at the two men.

"Oh Lord! It's Ned Sharpe's ghost!" gasps Noah, crossing himself and glancing up toward the gibbet on the hilltop.

"Aye lads," the rider laughs. "I've come to take my revenge and drag you off to hell!"

Bill, the guard, is not so easily frightened. He reaches into the sack at his feet and comes up holding a large rifle. Its barrel is made of brass and it bells out at the end like a trumpet.

"You are no more a ghost than I am," growls Bill, his fingers fumbling at the hammer of the blunderbuss.

There is a flash of powder, the crack of a gunshot and Bill hears a bullet whistle past his ear and bury itself in the carriage roof with a hollow thud.

"The next shot will be on target," says the rider, pulling out a second pistol and pointing it at Bill.

"Drop your weapon, or I shall dispatch you to Judgement Day."

Bill doesn't like being shot at and he glares defiantly back at the highwayman. His thumb is resting on the trigger of his own gun and it will only take a flick of his wrist to put the rider in his sights. The blunderbuss holds half a pound of lead shot and at this range it will take the rider's head clean off. Bill loaded the gun first thing this morning but he has not checked it all day and there is no telling what the rain and fog might have done to the powder. It's an even bet whether it will fire at all.

"Put down your gun," says the rider evenly. "I've no quarrel with you. It is your passengers gold I'll be taking, not yours."

Under the cloak the highwayman seems a slight figure. The pistol is held steady enough but it looks very large in the rider's small, gloved hand. Bill guesses that the robber is no more than a boy. He darts a sideways glance at Noah, who sits wide-eyed with terror, holding onto the reins for dear life.

Boy or not, the rider's gun is pointing straight at Bill's heart. He has no liking for Mr Periwigge and no wish to die to save the man's gold. With a curse, Bill lowers the blunderbuss and tosses it down between the shafts of the carriage, causing the harnessed horses to snort and stamp nervously.

"Very wise," says the rider. "Now, my fine gentlemen, if you will do as I ask then I promise that no harm will come to you. Please be good enough to step down from your perch and lie upon the ground."

When Noah and Bill are lying face down in the mud, the rider jumps nimbly from the saddle, steps up to the carriage and knocks at the door with the pistol butt.

"Open up!"

"Don't shoot me," cries Mr Periwigge bravely. "Spare my life!"

"Step out where I can see you and there'll be no need for anyone to die," calls the highwayman.

Mr Periwigge tumbles out of the door, a small leather suitcase clutched tightly to his chest.

"Hand me your valuables," says the highwayman, "and I can let you be on your way."

"Do you know who I am?" says Mr Periwigge in a quivering voice. "I am a personal friend of Squire Colby - the Magistrate. I am travelling tonight on his business. He will hear of this and - "

"I do not care if you're travelling on the business of the devil himself!" growls the highwayman. "Deliver me your valuables or I shall be forced to plug your heart with lead."

Mr Periwigge gulps. He is no hero but there will be hell to pay if he loses the package that he is carrying to Colby Hall, not to mention the small fortune he paid for it on the Squire's behalf. Still holding tightly to his suitcase with one hand, Mr Periwigge reaches into the pocket of his coat and draws out a tiny silver pistol. There is a powder flash and Mr Periwigge's hat and wig fly off his head. He gives a yelp and drops the suitcase and the silver pistol, which discharges itself at his feet with an unconvincing 'pop'.

"You couldn't wound a sparrow with that trinket," snaps the highwayman, putting the smoking pistol away and whipping out a third. "No more tricks. My next shot will be the end of you - make no mistake!" Mr Periwigge falls back against the carriage and slides slowly down to sit in the mud, his eyes fixed with horror on the smoking bullet hole in the middle of his fallen hat.

The highwayman pockets the silver pistol and relieves Mr Periwigge of a gold snuffbox and signet ring, before slashing open the case with a swiftly drawn knife. Mr Periwigge's silk shirts and undergarments are tossed out and the highwayman comes up holding a large leather bag that clinks in a most satisfying way. Mr Periwigge scowls at this but he says nothing.

The highwayman is about to cast the case aside when something else slips out; a package tied up in brown paper.

"That is of no use to you," says Mr Periwigge hastily, clearly more terrified at the thought of losing the parcel than he is of the highwayman's loaded pistol. "It is for Squire Colby and he will not be pleased to lose it."

"All the better," laughs the highwayman. "There is no man I would rather rob than Josia Colby!"

The paper is torn away to reveal a small, leather bound book with a binding of intricate gold leaf. On the cover of the book are engraved three keys, woven about with a wreath of leaves. In the dimness of the night the golden patterns flicker like living flames.

The highwayman stows the book safely away in the folds of the cloak.

"You'll hang for this!" says Mr Periwigge in a trembling voice.

"A good evening to you sir," replies the highwayman, with a bow. "Jack Shadow, at your service. Be careful how you go in the fog. It is easy to go astray on a night like this."

As the highwayman rides away into the mist, Mr Periwigge grabs up his mud-soaked wig and jams it hastily back onto his bald head. Bill and Noah are climbing warily to their feet and wiping the dirt from their clothes.

"Get after him, you gutless cowards!" he shouts.

The coachman shakes his head:

"I'm not taking a bullet from Jack Shadow, not for anyone." He has had quite enough of Mr Periwigge, of rain and mud and the wilds of Cornwall. He wants nothing more than to go back to Bristol and never leave the city again.

Mr Periwigge turns to the guard.

"You are supposed to protect me from the likes of that ruffian!"

Bill is in no hurry to face the dark rider again and by the time he has cleaned the mud from his blunderbuss and found his dry powder the sound of the galloping hooves has died away.

Bill might have felt differently about giving chase if he had seen what happened as the rider crossed Reavers Hill.

As the stallion breaks out of the fog onto the moonlit hilltop, a breeze lifts the rider's hat and sends it tumbling to the grass. A pale blue ribbon twists after the hat and the rider's long, chestnut hair falls down over her shoulders. Ruby Gilbert wheels the horse about and rides back. She jumps down, grabs up the hat and ribbon and leaps nimbly back up into the saddle, before turning the horse and galloping off once more, her eyes flashing with wild delight.

Down the hill she races, in a whirlwind of mist and rushing trees. The stallion runs sure-footed and Ruby knows the road so well that she could ride it blindfold. At the bottom of Reavers Hill they turn up the lane toward Bascome village. On the flat ground, Ruby urges the stallion into a reckless gallop and he springs forward, flying along the lane like a thunderbolt.

Ruby has never dared to ride the stallion through the village before. Normally she would escape across the moors or stay out of sight on a poacher's path but the fog hides them so well that it makes her bold. The danger of the robbery has passed and Ruby is in a tameless mood. It has been a good night; she has enough gold to feed her family for many months and she has robbed Squire Colby's messenger into the bargain!

They leap over the bridge by the inn and tear up the village street, the stallion's hooves thundering on the cobbles, the whitewashed houses slipping past in a blur. The coachman took Ruby for the ghost of a highwayman and now she flies like a phantom rider through the foggy village, making enough noise to wake the dead. Ruby laughs as she rides; let the wild galloping wake the whole village! Who among them - living or dead - would guess that the fearsome highwayman, Jack Shadow, is a girl of thirteen years old?

Chapter 2.

The corridors of Colby Hall twist and turn like a maze, making it all too easy to lose your way. The staircases wind up past empty landings where shadowed doors open into forgotten rooms. There are attics where only mice have set foot for a hundred years and bedrooms where only spiders sleep. There are silent libraries ankle deep in dust, lonely balconies, deserted ballrooms, galleries, moth-infested cupboards and dank cellars where nameless things rot in darkness.

  Lucy Cotton has only been working at the hall for a month, and she is usually lost, but she has never been lost in the middle of the night before, nor in such a desolate part of the house. The rooms that she finds herself in are filled with rotting furniture, the windows are broken and the floors are deep in dry leaves. With a shudder, Lucy realises that she has strayed into the old East Wing.

  A sudden gust of wind slams a door and the flame of Lucy's candle dances, sending shadows leaping up the walls. She shrieks and drops her tea tray with a crash. The candle falls with the tray, while Lucy stands as still as she can, her hands over her face, hardly daring to breathe. She has heard awful tales about the East Wing of Colby Hall.

"There was that servant girl who hung herself in the scullery," Ned, the stable boy, told her on her first day."She can't have been much older than you. A pretty little thing she was, but when they cut her down her tongue was black and her eyes bulged out like this . . . " Ned pulled a horrid face and laughed heartily at Lucy's reaction. "She couldn't be put in the cemetery on account of her being a suicide so they buried her in the rose garden in the dead of night. She still wanders the grounds, calling at the windows to be let back in.

"She won't be lonely," Ned said, leaning closer and dropping his voice to a whisper."There's plenty of other ghosts to keep her company. The worst of the lot is the shade of old Nathaniel Colby. He was the Squire's father. They say he made a pact with the devil. He lived for an unnatural long time and when he died his body just shrivelled up like a leaf. There was nothing left of him to bury but a handful of dust."

Lucy screws her eyes tighter and bites her lip. There are whispering voices all around her in the darkness and the ancient floorboards creak under the tread of phantom feet. From somewhere nearby comes the tap-tap-tap of fingernails on a window pane. Lucy wishes that she could shut her ears as tightly as she has her eyes.

For a long moment, nothing happens. The wind sighs in the trees and the branches rattle on the broken glass. Lucy takes a deep breath.
"There's no such thing as ghosts," She whispers to herself, only half believing it. "That nasty boy only told those tales to scare me." She thinks of how Ned would laugh if he could see her there, trembling with fear, and she resolves to be brave. "I can't stand here all night shivering like a ninny!"

Lucy opens her eyes a crack. By some miracle, her candle is still alight where it fell, propped up against the teapot among the ruins of the Squire's best china.

Lucy sets the candle back on the tray and begins to pick up as much of the broken crockery as she can find. The teapot handle has come off and most of the cups are broken. The shattered china is sharp and she cuts her finger, staining the white cloth of the tray with bright drips of scarlet. She tries not to think about the trouble she will be in when she gets back to the kitchen.

Holding the tray in her trembling hands, Lucy sets off once more. Colby Hall might be big but it does not go on forever. She is sure to find her way back somehow.

Soon enough, Lucy comes across footprints in the dust and turns to follow them, hoping that they will lead her back to a more inhabited part of the house. The footprints lead along a corridor hung with rotting tapestries and up a stair. The staircase winds up and up and Lucy is just considering turning back when she sees a light ahead. At the top of the stairs is a door with a line of yellow lamplight shining underneath.

From the room beyond comes the muffled sounds of a man's voice. The voice is deep and rhythmic, as if he is reciting a poem. Lucy starts forward with relief but then, remembering her place, she stops, dusts down her apron and knocks. Lost or not, she is still only a chambermaid.

The light goes out at once and the voice falls silent. Lucy waits. She is just lifting her hand to knock again when the door swings open.

The room is dim, lit only by the glow of Lucy's candle and a smudge of moonlight at the window at the far end. The walls are lined with books and there is a long table stretching the length of the chamber. There is a bitter smell in the air, like the scent of a smouldering lamp wick.
"Hello . . ." Lucy begins in a faltering voice." I'm sorry to bother you, sir, but I'm lost. Can you tell me the way back to the kitchen?"
There is no reply but the soft tick of a clock.

Lucy steps inside. On the table, on a cloth of black silk, lie the bones of a bird. They are laid out neatly, all in place, the hooked beak open and the wings spread. Next to the hawk's skeleton are several long jawed animal skulls, their cruel teeth glittering in the moonlight. Each skull bares a dark, rusty mark between its eyes. Further along the table stands a large, leather bound book with some curious pieces of burned paper between the pages. Lucy steps closer but she cannot understand the words written there. Beside the book is a knife and a silver bowl filled with dark liquid. There are pale shapes on the floor at Lucy's feet. Are they bones?

Something moves in the darkness beyond the table and Lucy lifts her gaze to see several pairs of large, yellow eyes watching her. The nearest pair of eyes begins to move toward her and a huge, shaggy shape steps from the shadows. As Lucy opens her mouth to scream a strong hand is clamped over her mouth.

Chapter 3.

Colby Hall rises above Bascome forest like a vast, turreted crag. Every window in the old house is dark - all save one, high in the tower of the crumbling East Wing.

Inside the tower room a black candle burns in an iron stand by the window, its light falling dimly upon the table top, leaving the rest of the chamber in darkness. The Sorcerer stands at the window, his shadow looming large in the candlelight, his face hidden by the hood of his black robe.

The Sorcerer opens the book and begins to chant:

"Hemlock, Fire and Viper's Tongue
Weasel Tooth and Graveyard Bone
Blight and Famine, Rot and Rust
Pestilence, Decay and Dust."

He reaches out and takes a handful of dust from the bowl and casts it into the candle flame.

"Come Ruin, come Thirst
Come Waste and Wither
Heed my call and hasten hither!"

The candle sputters out and a coil of black smoke rises. The smoke cloud seethes and swells, sending shadowy tendrils reaching out toward the hooded figure.

"Obey me, devouring spirits. I am your summoner!"

The smoke draws back, hissing and chattering, watching the sorcerer with lightless eyes.
"We are hungry," whisper the voices in the smoke.
The sorcerer steps to the window, flings it open and gestures away over the moonlit forest.
"Take your payment from Seth Gilbert's field," he commands." Lay it waste."
 Like an obedient dog, the smoke slinks silently over the windowsill and spills out into the night, rising up over the forest and flying down the valley toward Bascome village.

   Under the eaves of the cottage, Ruby Gilbert lies asleep in her tiny attic room, dreaming of riding wild horses in the moonlight. Her sister Katy is curled up in the bed beside her and in the room next door, their brother Tom snores on the unmade bed, his muddy boots still on his feet. Downstairs, Ruby's father, Seth Gilbert, lies on a narrow cot by the kitchen fire, dreaming a blindman's dream of his dear departed wife, Lizzie. Jet the sheepdog lies by the hearth with his head on his paws, dreaming of rabbits.

   The darkness sweeps down over Seth Gilbert's cottage, swirling about the roof and walls, withering the ivy, stripping the petals from the roses and turning the dew on the window panes to ice. It slips over the barn and down onto the acre of ploughed earth beyond.

    Unearthly voices whisper and shadowy shapes dart over the field. Frost sparkles on the cabbages and phantom hands reach out to brush the leaves of the turnips and potatoes. Soon, every flower in the field has wilted, the sap in every stem has frozen solid and every last root has shrivelled in the earth.

When all the life has been taken from the field, the dark cloud rises up and melts away into the night.

Chapter 4.

The mist has cleared and the moon has set, leaving the land dim in the starlight. The wolves leap up the hillside. They are huge and lean, their shaggy coats dark as rags torn from the night sky. They scale the bank beside the Bristol road and come to a halt at the top, surveying the scene below them with their slitted, yellow eyes. The fallen tree lies in the ditch where the coachmen left it and the roadway has been churned to mud by the carriage wheels. The wolves lift their snouts to taste the wind. They catch the scents of rum, tobacco, sweat and fear. They taste the sharp odours of gunpowder, rusty iron and damp leather, the smell of horses and of humans. The lead wolf jumps down the bank, finds the marks left by Ruby's boots and darts back and forth until he has hunted out her horse's track. He growls and sets off at a run toward the top of Reavers Hill, the rest of the pack swarming behind him.

The wolves pause to sniff at the place where Ruby stopped to pick up her hat, then race on, down the far side of the Hill and away up the valley. As the pack run through Bascome village, the dogs sense their passing; they stiffen in alarm but they make no sound, waiting in breathless terror for the dark wolves to pass.

Above the village, the stallion's trail turns away from the road and leads off into the trees. It is as dark as a dungeon below the eaves of the forest but the wolves have no need of light to find their way. The stallion's trail leads on, through a beech wood, over a mossy bank and down into the bed of a stream.

The wolves halt at the bank, their hackles rising, snarling at the running water, pacing back and forth with their tails twitching. The stream is neither deep nor swift but the ancient magic of running water forbids the fell beasts from crossing.

The wind gusts up and a smoke of storm clouds sweep the stars from the sky. There is a rumble of thunder and sudden rain falls like a second darkness. Raindrops hiss down into the stream and the lead wolf steps back with a growl. He turns away and leads the pack downstream.

The wolves find a fallen tree making a bridge over the water and, one by one, they step along the tree trunk and double back up the stream, their snouts low to the earth, hunting for scent. The storm sweeps on, carrying the rain inland, leaving Bascome valley to glisten darkly in the starlight. The forest floor is still dry enough to carry a trail but at the edge of the wood, where the fields rise toward Colby Hall, the rainstorm has washed the stallion's hoof marks clean away. The wolves mill about, sniffing and pawing at the earth, but the scent is gone.

The lead wolf sits back on his haunches, lifts his face to the stars, and howls. The rest of the pack follow suit, raising their voices in an unearthly chorus. The forest falls still, hunting owls turn on the wing and flee, while foxes, weasels and scuttling mice hunch down on the earth and wait for the awful sound to end. They know that evil is abroad in the forest; the howl is a cry of hatred for all living things.

At Colby Hall, the human sleepers are shivered awake, their ears ringing with the last strains of the terrible cry. Mr Periwigge whimpers, buries his head under his blanket and jams his fingers into his ears. In the cottage at the top of Gilbert's lane, far off down the valley, Ruby Gilbert turns over in her sleep. The wolves' distant call is too faint to wake her but it reaches into her dream, darkening the stars and sending a shiver down her spine.

Chapter 5.

Ruby sits on a mossy boulder beside the Folly Brook watching the trout moving lazily in the sun dappled water at her feet, their scales glimmering in the shadows like pieces of a fallen rainbow. The trees grow thick here, hiding her from all sides. Ruby's mother first showed her the glade when she was a little girl and it has been her secret place ever since.

Ruby reaches into her pocket and takes out the book that she stole from Mr Periwigge. The gold leaf on the binding flashes in the sunlight as she opens it:

"The Keys of Queen Mab. The mysteries of her kingdom and her magic, written by the hand of one who has visited her realm.

Many have searched for the path into Faerie but few find it. Only the pure of heart may hope to pass its gates and return unscathed and none return unchanged. The Twilight land lies very near to the Waking World. There are many gates yet it is most difficult to reach. It is a place of great beauty and terrible peril."

What would the Squire want with a book of Fairy Tales? Ruby leafs through the book, watching the light flicker on the gold edges of the pages. She stops at random and reads more:

"The Hounds of Queen Mab:
Long ago, Queen Mab made these beasts to be her servants. They are seven in number and they

resemble wolves, though they are larger than any mortal wolf and their coats are dark as a sunless night. These creatures were once men and they retain the souls and wits of men and have a speech all of their own that is awful to hear. Their voices may be used to cast enchantment upon the minds of mortals and it is for this that they are named the Witch Wolves -"

Ruby is startled from her reading by the sound of voices. She puts the book away in her pocket and goes to investigate.

Two men are climbing the path toward the hilltop. One is a lumbering giant of a man, dressed in a grey soldier's coat, the other is slight and furtive, with a ratty face and long greasy hair. They are too far off for Ruby to hear what they were saying but she recognises them at once; they are Squire Colby's men. Whatever they are up to, it cannot be good. Ruby hides the book in a hollow tree and sets off up the hill after the two men, taking care to remain well hidden.

Davey Tachard stands at the edge of the wood, watching the skylark riding the wind over Bascome valley. The little bird bobs in the breeze, its music ringing out over the hillside. As he listens, a poem begins to form in his mind. He sits down on the grass and takes his notebook, pen and ink from the pocket of his coat. Dipping the nib of the quill into the ink, he begins to write.

Davey is so engrossed in his writing that he does not hear the sound of approaching feet. The crack of a dry twig startles him but he turns too late to avoid the kick that sends him sprawling onto his face.
A harsh voice rings out:
"Grab him!"
Davey rolls to his feet just in time to avoid an outstretched hand. He bats the arm away, steps back and raises his fists.

The man who had tried to grab Davey is huge. He wears a grey coat, faded blue cavalryman's trousers and a sword at his belt. He is as bald as an egg, with a heavy featured, pockmarked face. The large man's companion is a short, ratty man, with long, greasy hair and a poisonous smile.
"You're a game young pup," says the rat faced man."Perhaps you fancy going a round of fisticuffs with Captain Ransome?" He glances over at the bald man, who grins nastily and folds the hairy fingers of his right hand into a fist.
"What's wrong boy - cat got your tongue?" growls the grey-coated giant.
Davey guesses that it must have been Rat Face who had knocked him down. If the big man had kicked him, he would have broken Davey's spine. The man's clenched fist is almost as big as Davey's head.
"You're trespassing," says the little man with a sneer. "Squire Colby doesn't take kindly to that."
"I thought that the Squire's land ended on the other side of the village," says Davey.
"This whole valley will be Squire Colby's before long." The man glances at the scattered papers and back up

at Davey. "There's not many people in this backwater that can read. I reckon you must be the Vicar's boy, David Tachard, back from school in Bristol?" He smiles at Davey's look of surprise.

"You know who I am," says Davey. "But I don't know your name."

"Oh - pardon me!" sneers Rat Face, giving Davey a mocking bow. "Allow me to introduce myself: I am Mr Furey and this is my colleague, Captain Ransome, and we are Squire Colby's business partners."

Davey nods, feeling a chill of fear; Mr Furey and Captain Ransome are the Squire's hired thugs, ruthless men whose job it is to intimidate anyone who stand in Josia Colby's way. There was talk of little else in the village these days; how the Squire was turning the farmers out of their homes so that he could mine tin. The mines were appearing everywhere, the slag heaps scarring the land, their tall chimneys belching out smoke.

"Many things have changed while you've been away at school, Master Tachard," says Mr Furey.

"Not much of it for the better," replies Davey.

Mr. Furey steps forward and crushes Davey's fallen pen under his boot. "It was careless of you to leave that there. You ought to take more care with your words too. We've ways of sorting out cheeky runts like you." He gives a sideways glance toward his companion. "I think this lad needs a lesson in manners?"

Captain Ransome nods.

Davey has tangled with enough bullies to know that he only has two choices; fight or run. If they were boys of his own age then he might stand a chance but these are grown men. Captain Ransome has his sword and Mr Furey has a knife at his belt. Davey glances down at the spilled papers on the grass. His book of poems is too precious to be left behind.

Davey moves fast. He sidesteps, as if he were trying to run past Captain Ransome, then swerves quickly back, darting his hand down to grab the book. Captain Ransome is fooled and sent lumbering away in the wrong direction but sharp-eyed Mr Furey spots the trick at once. He swipes out with his foot, catching Davey on the ankle and tripping him up. The little man throws himself onto Davey's back, pinning him down and grabbing his throat. Davey jabs back with his elbow, hitting Mr Furey in the face and the man falls off with a yelp of pain. He is up again at once.

"Get the boy!" he hisses.

Davey springs away but he is not quick enough. Captain Ransome's hand closes over his arm and hauls him back. He takes Davey's wrists in a crushing grip and twists both of his arms back in their sockets. Davey struggles but it is no use.

Mr Furey rubs his hand over his bruised cheek and glares at Davey.

"You'll pay for that," he mutters. "And you'll learn to respect me. Hold him, Ransome. I want to get a good swing at him."

Mr Furey takes a billy club from the pocket of his coat. A handful of lead shot wrapped in leather, the club is a small but vicious weapon.

"I think I'll start by knocking this puppy's teeth out," he says, slapping the billy club down into his palm and smiling nastily.
As Captain Ransome's grip tightens, Davey closes his eyes and waits for the first blow to fall.

Davey feels a swish of air against his cheek, followed by a dull thud.
"What the blazes!?" Mr Furey exclaims.
Davey opens his eyes to see Mr Furey looking down at his coat with a bemused expression on his face. His chest is covered in brown mush which, from the smell of it it, could only be cow dung. There is another wet thud and Captain Ransome gives a jerk. He throws Davey to the floor and spins about.

Davey rolls to his knees and turns to see the big man wiping thick dung from the back of his head. Most of the cow pat has gone down the neck of his coat. There is a rustle from the hedge and third missile comes flying, hitting Mr Furey full in the face. There is a laugh from the bushes and a cheeky voice rings out:
"There's plenty more where that came from, you daft maggots!"
With a roar of rage, Captain Ransome leaps forward, crashing the branches aside. Mr Furey is only a few steps behind, wiping the dung from his eyes and spitting curses. Laughter rings out among the trees, but it is soon drowned out by the sound of the two men blundering through the bushes.

Davey gets to his feet. His coat is torn but he is otherwise unhurt. He gathers up his things and sets off along the edge of the wood. He hopes that the mysterious cow pat thrower can run fast.

Davey has almost reached the road and is peering about for any sign of the Squire's thugs when he hears voice behind him:
"Aren't you going to thank me?"
Davey spins around to meet the amused gaze of Ruby Gilbert.
"Was that you?"
Ruby shrugs. "It didn't look like a fair fight to me. I thought I'd even things up."
"What if they'd caught you?"
Ruby grins and pushes a loose strand of brown hair back into her pony tail.
"I'm not afraid of those lackwits. Besides, there's plenty of places to hide in the wood, if you know what you're doing."
Davey stares at Ruby. He has hardly seen her in the last three years and in that time she had grown from a mischievous girl into a spirited young woman.
"What are you looking at me like that for?" says Ruby, narrowing her eyes and smiling again.
Davey reddens and looks down at his boots, feeling suddenly foolish. She has always managed to make him feel this way, defensive and sort of stupid and giddy, all at the same time.
"What's that book?" Ruby asks, nodding down at the notebook that Davey still holds tight in his hand.
"You were willing to risk a beating to keep it - it must be good."
"It's nothing," Davey shrugs.

"Let me see," says Ruby, playfully tugging the book from Davey's grasp. She has always teased him, ever since they were knee high, running about under the stalls in the market square. They are both thirteen now and the teasing is charged with something sharper.

Davey tries to grab the book back but Ruby jumps back out of his reach, laughing. She opens the journal.

"A poem?" she says. "The Skylark."
She reads:

"Where comes the rising song so fair?
Spun like gold upon the air
Sky harp, herald of the spring
Rise to heaven's vault and sing
For beggar, shepherd boy and king
To all, your windblown beauty bring.

"I like the bit about the gold on the air," she says, raising her eyes. "That's just how a Skylark sounds."
"It's not finished," Davey mumbles, taking the book back.
"You know about books, don't you?"
"A bit."
"I've some things of my mother's." Ruby looks down at her hands, not trusting her face to lie. "There's an old book I want to sell but the pawn broker in Truro is a weasel. Could you tell me if it's worth anything?"
"I'll have a look at it," Davey says. "I'm going to Truro myself on Saturday. Farmer Finch is riding there in his wagon - you could come with us."

"Perhaps," says Ruby, smiling.
A voice comes through the trees:
"Ruby!"
"That's Katy," she says. "I'd better go and see what she wants."

Ruby would like nothing better than to walk through the woods with Davey but there is an urgency in Katy's calling. Besides that, there are a hundred things to be done this morning. There's bread to be fetched and clean washing to be taken back up to Mrs Carrick - Jack Shadow or not, Ruby has to keep up appearances. With a last look over her shoulder at Davey, Ruby sets off for home.

Katy is waiting at the gate of Gilbert's cottage.
"Come and look!" says Katy breathlessly, her brown eyes wide with concern. "Everything's died."
"What's died?"
"In the field!"
Ruby follows Katy past the cottage to where Seth Gilbert is kneeling on the ground with a pile of shrivelled leaves in his hands. As Ruby rushes to her father's side she sees that the field that Seth had planted so carefully that spring has withered from end to end.
"Katy say's the whole lot's blighted?" says Seth. He turns his blind eyes toward Ruby, hoping that she will tell him a different story.
Ruby has never seen anything like it. The surrounding hedgerows are still green and bright with blooming wildflowers but it is as if winter has fallen on the field, killing everything. Every leaf is

withered, every stem cracked and dry and it is cold here, despite the sunshine.
"Katy's right," Ruby says softly. "It's all gone."
"It's not natural," mutters Seth."Not in June." He lets the dry leaves fall and the wind catches them and sends them spinning up into the blue sky. He turns his face away, not wanting his daughters to see the tears in his eyes

A magpie flies down from the hedge to perch on a withered stem and turns its head about, surveying the ruined field. It gives a disdainful croak and flies off again, its tail feathers shimmering with dark rainbows. Ruby shivers. There is something very wrong here. Frost does not come at midsummer and a whole acre of land does not wither overnight.
"One for sorrow, two for mirth, three for a - " Katy begins to sing, but Ruby motions for her to be quiet.
"You go and check the hens," she says, giving Katy's hand a squeeze. "We'll have eggs for breakfast."
Katy nods and runs to the chicken pen, glad to have something to do.
"It can't be helped," Ruby says, putting a hand on her father's shoulder. "We'll make do somehow. I can always take in more washing."
"Perhaps we should sell the cottage, after all," mutters Seth. "The Squire is eager enough to get his hands on our land. We could move into the village -"
"We're not beaten yet!" says Ruby. "This is our home!"
Ruby takes her father's arm. Normally he would shrug her off if she tried to help him but he leans on

her now and allows her to lead him back to the kitchen door.

"I'll go to Truro on market day and sell some more of Mam's treasures," says Ruby. She will be selling other things to the pawnbroker. The lie tastes bitter but Jack Shadow is Ruby's secret - no-one else can ever know.

"You won't sell the Kern?" says Seth sharply.

"Of course not, " Ruby squeezes her father's arm reassuringly as her other hand goes up to touch the pendant at her neck, a galloping horse, cast in bronze. Ruby has worn the Kern ever since her seventh birthday. It is an ancient thing, passed down from mother to daughter from time out of mind. Worn smooth by countless hands, the Kern nestles in the hollow of Ruby's palm like a seawashed pebble, reminding her every day of her mother.

"They say it brings luck, especially with horses," her mother told her, as she fastened it about Ruby's neck on its silver chain. The Kern has hung there ever since. No matter how desperate she is, Ruby knows that she will never sell it.

"Sam Finch told me that he wants you to go and look at a sick mare," says Ruby. "He always pays well."

"He'll only pay if I can cure the beast," says Seth.

"Don't talk daft, dad. You're still the finest stableman in Cornwall. Everyone knows that."

Seth says nothing. Three years ago, perhaps, that might have been true, but what use is he now? Ever since the accident that left him blind, a curse has fallen over his life.

"You can hitch Bess up to the plow and Tom can help you sew the field again," says Ruby as brightly as she can. "We can still have some crops by the autumn."
"You're a good lass." Seth straightens his back and forces himself to smile.

Ruby is more concerned about her father's wounded pride than the withered crops. She will sell the ring that she took from Mr Periwigge. That, along with the other money she has hidden away, will be more than enough to see them through the winter.

Chapter 6.

Ruby pushes open the door of the inn and steps inside, a basket of clean washing balanced on her hip. Katy comes behind her, peering shyly from her sister's side into the dim interior of the White Horse. "The coachman was in here last night," Mrs Carrick is saying, to anyone who will listen, "and he told me himself how Jack Shadow threatened to murder them all!" Mrs Carrick is a plump, red-faced woman with a bustling manner. Her inn is half full, busy for a lunchtime, and buzzing with conversation. The White Horse is always the best place in the village to hear the latest gossip. "I don't know what the world is coming to, when decent folks can't go about their business without being held up at gunpoint."
"Its safe enough for the likes of us," laughs Tad Willow, his gangly frame propping up the bar. "Jack Shadow only robs those as have more money than sense, the sort who've stolen it in the first place or got rich off the backs of others." Tad raises his tankard. "If Jack Shadow were here now, I'd drink his health."
"Heaven forbid!" tuts the scandalised landlady. "He's nothing but a murdering ruffian, just like old Ned Sharpe. "
"Ned Sharpe may have been a rogue," replies Tad, "but did you ever hear of Jack Shadow killing a man? He's a gentleman I tell you, our new Robin Hood."
Mrs Carrick smiles when she sees Ruby and Katy standing in the doorway and hurries over to take Ruby's basket of washing.

"Have you heard about last night?" she begins, happy to have another opportunity to tell the tale. "It's too awful for words..."

Ruby and Katy are told the story of the robbery on Reavers Hill, recounted in lurid and fantastic detail, followed by all the other local scandal.
"They say that the kitchen maid ran off from Colby Hall last night. The Squire will have no servants left before long. It's no wonder. That hall is a nasty place. And there's that little lad gone missing from the farmhouse up on Beggars Moor - "
"That's three children that have been taken in as many months," puts in Tad Willow.
"What do you mean, taken?" says Mrs. Carrick. "The poor thing probably just wandered off and fell down a mine shaft."
"There's things been seen up on the moors," says Tad. "Great black beasts that come to the lonely farmhouses in the night and steal away the lambs. When they can't get lambs they carry off the children."
"Moonshine!" scolds Mrs.Carrick." I'll not have you scaring young Katy with your silly tales."

When they have heard all of Mrs. Carrick's gossip, and the innkeeper's wife has paid Ruby for the washing with a loaf of bread and round of cheese, Ruby and Katy make their way home. The hedges lining the lane from Bascome are full of honeysuckle, dogrose and poppies and Katy runs ahead, clambering up to pick blossoms for a posy. Ruby walks slowly behind; hearing the talk of Jack

Shadow's exploits has made her thoughtful. She felt a thrill of pride as Tad Willow raised his toast but the story that Mrs. Carrick told bore little relation to the events as they had actually happened. People see what they want to see, Ruby supposes. Jack Shadow could be a ruthless murderer, a thief or a hero. His reputation has served her well enough but there is danger in it too.

"What's that?" asks Katy, startling Ruby from her thoughts. She is pointing up into the hedge beside the road.

The sheltered lane runs behind high hedged banks but a small patch of leaves are rustling. Ruby puts down her basket and pushes aside the branches. There is a blur of movement and an agonised cheeping sound.

The sparrow struggles frantically but his leg is caught fast in a cleft twig and his wings are snagged on the thorns. The bird gives a last flutter and goes limp, closing his eyes and drawing his head down into his ruffled neck feathers. Ruby reaches into the hedge and gently takes the sparrow in her hand. She teases the thorns from his wings, presses apart the twig that holds his leg and pulls him free.

The bird lies still on her hand.

"Is he dead?" asks Katy.

Ruby can feel the soft thrum of the tiny heart beating fast against her palm.

"Just frightened."

Katy leans closer and sees the delicate feathers at the Sparrow's breast quivering.

The bird opens his eyes and shakes his wings. He hops up and perches on Ruby's finger, blinking his shiny, coal black eyes and darting his beak down to pull his tangled feathers into place. All of a sudden he flinches and cowers down in Ruby's hand.

Ruby looks up. A hawk sits on a branch high above, half hidden in the shadows. The hawk's feathers are storm grey and its beak and talons are black. Its attention has been fixed upon the sparrow but now it raises its narrow head to glare at Ruby.

"I don't like it," whispers Katy."It wants to kill the sparrow."

As if in reply, the bird opens its beak wide and hisses. The cry is so unexpected and so filled with malice that Ruby feels the hairs at the back of her neck stand on end. Katy scowls and bends down to pick up a stone from the road.

"Go away, you nasty thing!" she shouts, raising her hand to throw.

The hawk hurls itself down from the branch with a shriek, flying at Ruby like an arrow, its talons reaching for her eyes. Ruby ducks just in time to avoid being blinded and feels the wind from the hawk's wings whip her cheek as it shoots past her head. She catches the foul stink of rotting carrion as the hawk swoops away along the lane and soars up out of sight over the trees.

The sparrow flutters up onto a nearby branch and bobs about nervously, checking to see if the coast is clear. Satisfied, it gives a loud chirrup and flies off over the hedge

"He said Thank You" smiles Katy.

The wind has a chill in it now and Ruby can see clouds rolling in from the sea, bruised and dark with rain. As they hurry on, Katy begins to complain about her worn out shoes and Ruby lifts her up and carries her on her shoulders.

They are at the bottom of Gilbert's lane when they hear the clatter of hooves on the road behind them. Ruby puts Katy down on the bank and steps aside to let the rider pass.

"Good afternoon Miss Gilbert," says Squire Colby, reining in his horse. He is a tall man, middle aged and well built but showing no sign of softening at the edges. His face is narrow and strong featured and his thick, black hair is peppered with grey.

Katy moves closer to Ruby and scowls up at Josia Colby. She knows who he is and she knows that she does not like him one bit.

"Good afternoon, Squire Colby," replies Ruby, nodding politely and turning away.

The man urges his horse forward to keep pace with her.

"There's no need to rush off," he says. " You act as if you don't wish to be seen talking to me."

Ruby looks up to meet the Squire's dark eyes.

"I meant no offence, sir, I'm sure, but I have plenty of things to do today. We are not all fortunate enough to be gentlemen of leisure."

"You would have an easier life up at the Hall," says the Squire, leaning forward and resting his arms on the pommel of his saddle. The green stone in his silver signet ring glimmers in the stormy light like a drop of poison. "Have you thought about the offer that I made you? We are still in need of a chambermaid."

Ruby's cheeks flush and her eyes spark with anger but she holds back the words that she wants to spit into the Squire's face. She would rather beg in the street than work for Squire Colby. "I've nothing more to say to you. Good day."

Ruby steps away but the Squire simply kicks his horse forward, blocking their path.

"You're a headstrong lass," he says, reaching down and grabbing Ruby's hand. She throws him off and steps further back. "Your father should know better than to work you so hard - you're too pretty to have such rough hands."

Ruby is too angry to speak. She pulls Katy tighter to her, her face hardening with fury. If only she had her pistols. She would make him dance to a different tune then!

The Squire misreads Ruby's silence for fear, and leans forward, softening his voice. "You wouldn't have starve up at the manor, Ruby, and your sister could wear decent shoes on her feet. I might even think about giving your father his old job back." The Squire is a patient man, when he has to be, and used to getting his own way. "It's really not safe living up there on the edge of the moor. What would you do if that villain Jack Shadow turned up on your doorstep?"

"We're not afraid of him," Ruby snarls. She keeps her face fierce, but inside she is laughing - If he only knew the truth! "Jack Shadow only troubles the likes

of you. I heard that it was your errand boy he robbed last night?"
Squire Colby meets Ruby's furious gaze with one of his own. "You don't want to go the way of your mother," the Squire says, his voice filled with quiet menace. "Working your way into an early grave - that would be such a waste." He reaches out suddenly and grabs Ruby's arm again, pulling her hard up against the horse's flank. He leans forward and speaks into her ear. "Your fields will wither, your livestock will die and then, when you are starving, you will come crawling to me on your knees like a dog."
The Squire's grip is like iron and his eyes smoulder with such sudden hatred that Ruby catches her breath. Seeing that he has finally frightened her, Josia Colby smiles. He gives Ruby's arm a parting twist and flings her back into the hedge. Then he digs in his heels and wheels the horse round, passing so close to Ruby that she has to scramble out of the way to avoid being kicked.

Ruby stands glaring after him, her heart thumping the way little sparrow's had done only a moment before. The Squire's threat has shaken her - how had he known about the field? Damn him! If it wasn't for Josia Colby, then her mother would still be alive and her father would still have his sight.

Seth Gilbert was the Squire's chief stableman, until the fateful day when Josia Colby whipped his prize stallion until it had bled, furious that the horse had proved too strong willed to let him ride it. The Squire pushed Seth into the stall to tend to Caliban's wounds while the beast was still maddened with pain and the stallion attacked him at once. By some miracle, Ruby's father survived but a kick from Caliban's hooves left him blind.

Ruby's mother did her best to support the family after that but, a year later, worn down by worry, Lizzie Gilbert took ill and died. With her mother gone and her father blind, it fell to Ruby to hold the family together.

Katy is sobbing and clinging to Ruby's side, her face buried in Ruby's dress, her posy of flowers lying on the mud, trampled by the Squire's horse. Ruby shrugs off her fury as best she can and picks her sister up. "He's gone now," she says gently. "There's nothing to worry about."

Ruby is about to turn up Gilbert's lane but she stops in her tracks when she sees the grey hawk, perched on a branch on the other side of the lane, watching her intently. She catches the graveyard stink again and notices how thin and ragged the hawk is - more like the corpse of a bird than a living creature. With a sickening jolt she realises that she can see bare bone at the back of the creatures empty eye sockets. The creature has no eyes!

Ruby goes cold. There is a sense of wrongness about everything now, as if the balance of nature has been tampered with. It is the same feeling that came over her this morning as she stood by her father's withered field, but far stronger. As Ruby stares into the deathly emptiness of the hawk's eye sockets the air about her seems to thicken. Cracks open in the shadows and darkness spills out, choking all the joy and light from the world.

The sun comes out from behind the clouds and Ruby is dazzled. There is a rustle of leaves and the hawk is on the wing. Blinking, she turns her head to follow the hawk's flight through the trees.

Did that actually happen or did she imagine it? The vision of horror lasted only for the space of a heartbeat but it was utterly chilling. Ruby looks down at Katy, bundled into her arms, her head buried in Ruby's shoulder.

"Did you see the hawk?" she asks.

Katy shakes her head. "I'm cold," she says. "I want to go home."

Ruby sets off once again. The hill is steep and she has Katy and the basket to carry but the climb does not warm Ruby up. Her bones are like ice.

From a shadowed perch, high in the trees, the grey hawk watches Ruby with its empty eyes. It watches until she is out of sight, then it unfurls its grey wings and flies back along the road in the direction of Colby Hall.

Chapter 7.

Ruby is pushing open the front gate of Gilbert's cottage when a sudden explosion of sound rings out - a crash of shattering glass and a shout. There comes the sounds of a woman weeping and a man laughing. It's coming from the Tithe cottages, down the hill through the trees.

Ruby sets Katy down and takes the bread and cheese from her basket.
"Take these to Dad and tell him they are for his lunch," she says. "I'm going to see what's going on."
Katy trots up to the cottage and Ruby sets off at a run through the wood, filled with a sense of foreboding.

A cart stands in the middle of the neat front garden of widow Marsh's cottage. The horse is churning up the flower beds with its hooves and the cart wheels have made a dark gash across the little patch of lawn. The widow sits on the doorstep, weeping. At her feet lie the fragments of a glass vase. Leaning against the garden wall is Mr Furey, watching with amusement as Captain Ransome hauls an armchair toward the back of the cart.
"Accidents will happen," says Mr Furey. "I suggest you stay out of the way and let us get on with it. We are experts at removals."
Captain Ransome laughs and throws the armchair into the cart with a crash.
"What do you think you're doing?" blazes Ruby, pushing past Mr Furey to stand beside widow Marsh.

"The Squire's told us we are all evicted," says the widow through her tears. "He's put the rents up so high that none of us can afford them."

"She has lived in this cottage her whole life," says Ruby. "You can't just throw her out with no warning."

"It's all quite legal and above board, young lady," says Mr Furey. "There is an eviction notice fixed to the door, signed by the Magistrate."

Ruby turns to look along the row of cottages. White paper notices are nailed to all the doors. She reaches up and tears down the notice nailed to widow Marsh's front door.

"I should be careful, if I were you," says Mr Furey, his voice edged with steel. "Interfering with an Officer of the Law is a serious offence."

"You're an Officer of Nothing and your master is a criminal!" Ruby snaps. She studies the notice, reading it twice over to be sure of what it says. The signature at the bottom is no surprise: Josia Colby.

"I wouldn't want to hurt anyone as pretty as you," says Mr Furey, in a tone that implies quite the opposite. "But if you choose to obstruct the course of justice, then we may have to be forceful."

Captain Ransome sniggers.

"Don't make trouble for yourself on my account," says the Widow, taking Ruby's arm. "There's no use in it."

"Have you read this?" Ruby asks, holding the notice up for the widow to look at.

"I never learned to read . . ." falters the old lady.

Ruby turns to face the two thugs.

"It says that the tenants have until midday on the day following the posting of the notice to pay the rent in full. You can't evict anyone until tomorrow."

Mr Furey spits on the ground at Ruby's feet.

"A day here or there makes no odds," he mutters. "The old witch will be just as poor tomorrow as she is today."

"And just as homeless," puts in Captain Ransome with smirk.

Ruby stands firm. These fools don't scare her.

"If you evict anyone today then you'll be breaking the law. Squire Colby may think he is Lord and Master of this valley but the Justice in Truro won't be pleased to hear about any more illegal evictions. I'll ride and tell him myself if you don't leave at once."

"You'll have trouble riding anywhere with a broken head," says Captain Ransome.

"You have no idea who you are dealing with!" snarls Ruby.

The big man is taken aback at the sudden fire in Ruby's eyes and he turns to Mr Furey for guidance. Mr Furey glares coldly at Ruby. "We know who exactly you are, Miss Gilbert and we know where you live. You and your family will be the next to go."

"You can't evict us. My father owns the land that our cottage stands on."

Mr Furey smiles. "It's been a hot summer," he says softly, "and I'll bet the thatch on your cottage roof is as dry as tinder. One little spark is all it would take . . ." he leaves the threat hanging in the air.

"She's a trouble maker," growls Captain Ransome. "We should sort her out right now."

"Bide your time, Ransome," says Mr Furey, putting a restraining hand on the big man's arm. A crowd has gathered at the end of the garden path. The tenants of the other cottages, too frightened to raise their voices until now, have come to listen and the sight of Ruby's boldness has made them braver:

"If you harm her, then you'll answer to me," comes a man's voice. Several other voices, men's and women's, shout in agreement. Two of the men have axes in their hands.

Mr Furey turns to the crowd. "If any of you scum are left here tomorrow then I will make you wish you'd never been born!" he yells. "We will throw you and your dirty brats into the road without a stitch on your backs and take everything you own and burn it before your eyes." He turns back to Ruby with a sneer. "Happy now? You can't play the hero here, Missy. The more vexed you make me, the worse it will be for them. These cottages will be emptied and that's the end of it." Mr Furey steps toward Ruby and there comes a murmur of anger from the crowd. "I'll not forget you. And I'll enjoy teaching you a thing or too about respect, the next time we meet."

"I'd like to see you try," says Ruby, meeting his gaze evenly.

"Get the cart, Ransome," says Mr Furey, turning away from Ruby with a snarl. "We'll be back to deal with this lot tomorrow."

"You're a brave soul, Ruby," says widow Marsh, "and I'm glad that somebody stood up against those

villains, but I'm afraid for you. You don't want to make an enemy of Josia Colby."
"He is already my enemy," says Ruby.

The day is still sunny but the beauty of it is spoiled. The thought of the widow Marsh with no home fills Ruby with rage. Squire Colby behaves as if he owns the whole valley and everyone in it. No-one dares to stand against him - no-one but Jack Shadow.

The path back up to Gilbert's Cottage is steep and the hard walking helps Ruby to think more clearly. By the time she is home, she has the beginnings of a plan; it will be risky, but if it succeeds then Widow Marsh and the others will be able to stay in their cottages. Ruby smiles at the thought of how much her scheme will madden Squire Colby. Let him believe what he likes - he is not invincible.

Chapter 8.

The kitchen of Gilbert's cottage is cosy with firelight. Seth sits in his armchair by the hearth and Ruby sits at the table, sorting through the clothes to be mended. Tom sits opposite, with Seth's Flintlock rifle in front of him. Ruby watches Tom as he works, carefully cleaning each of the parts, oiling them and slipping them back together. Her brother can do anything that he sets his mind to, if he has a reason.

"Squire Colby has set his sights on finding Jack Shadow," says Tom. "There's a whole company of soldiers coming to the valley to hunt for him."

Ruby catches her breath and makes herself look down again at her sewing, avoiding Tom's eye.

"They wouldn't know where to start," she says, as calmly as she can manage.

"He's most likely got a den on the moors," says Tom, "but he'll have to come down and spend his loot. Someone's bound to spot him. The Squire's put a price of fifty guineas on his head - that's enough to loosen anyone's tongue."

"If you knew who Jack Shadow was," Ruby asks softly, "would Fifty Guineas be enough for you to sell him to the hangman?"

"Not me!" Tom replies hotly. "I'm no Trooper's Snitch. But you know how gold can turn a man's head."

What Tom says is true enough; it is one of the chief reasons that Ruby has worked so hard to keep her secret.

"I'd join Jack Shadow in an instant," says Tom. "I'd like nothing better than to rob a few rich gents and line my pockets with gold."

"It's not something to joke about," said Seth sternly. "This family's lost enough already without you getting yourself hung for a robber."

Tom clatters the rifle down on the table and turns to reply but Ruby kicks him in the shin and glares at him; the last thing she wants is for her brother to pick another argument with Seth. Tom scowls at Ruby but he holds his tongue. He is a year older than her but since their mother died Ruby has taken on the role of elder sister.

The tense mood is dispelled by Katy, as she gets up from the hearth and climbs onto her father's lap. "Tell me a story," she says.

Ruby goes back to her sewing and Tom bends back over the rifle, winding a rag about a stick to clean the soot from the inside of the barrel.

"Did you ever hear of Wayland Smith?" Seth begins.

"Is he the one who made Ruby's bronze horse?"

"That's what your mother always said," replies Seth. Ruby smiles; Lizzie Gilbert had often spoken of how the Kern had been made by Wayland Smith in the palace of Queen Mab. It was supposed to protect its wearer from all harm, to give them the power to tame wild horses and make sure that they never fell from the saddle. Ruby does not need any sort of magic to help her stay on a horse's back but she likes the tales all the same

"Was Wayland Smith like John Summer in the Village?" asks Katy.

"He was a blacksmith like John, " says Seth, "but he was more than that; he was a magician and a friend of the Faerie folk. He lived in a cave up on the moor, the one that we call Smith's Den. He knew all there was to know about metal craft and magic and even went to visit the Queen of the Faeries in her palace under the earth."

"Why does the Queen of the Faeries live underground?" asks Katy. "Isn't it dark down there?"

"The land of Faerie is lit by lanterns that hang from the roots of the tallest trees in our world. The lanterns shine like stars and make it always twilight."

"Who keeps all the lanterns burning?"

"Queen Mab has servants who can change into birds and animals. It's they who fly up to tend the fires in the star lanterns. She also sends her servants up to our world to spy on us. They say that if you can catch hold of a Faery animal and don't let go, it will take you back to Queen Mab's land. It's a dangerous thing to do. Those that come back from Faerie have mostly lost their wits."

"Did Wayland Smith lose his wits?"

"Not him - he was too smart. He knew how to pay the gatekeeper."

"What did he pay him?"

"He gave up the most precious thing he owned. That's the only way to be sure of coming home if you ever set foot on the road to Faerie -"

"But what was it?"

"You'll find out if you ever let me begin the story!"

Katy lays her head on her father's chest and Seth goes on with his tale.

Before long, Katy is asleep on her father's lap. Seth smiles, lifts her up in his arms and carries her up the stairs, not needing his sight to know the way in the house that he has lived in all his life.

When Ruby goes up to bed, she finds a folded sheet of paper on her dressing table, weighted down with a large pine cone. It is a poem about a skylark. The poet has not signed his work but he has left his muddy bootprints on the floor by the open window.

Ruby glances over at Katy, fast asleep under the blankets. She takes her cloak from the back of the door and steps to the window. A moment later she is climbing down the cottage wall. She jumps to the ground with practiced ease, slips away through the gate and out into the wood. She has left her pistols behind; for now, she is not Jack Shadow, she is simply herself - Ruby Gilbert - running through the starlight with a light heart.

She crosses the Folly Brook by the stepping stones, pausing at the far side to fill her pockets with pebbles, then runs down through the trees to the lane. The moon has not yet risen and in the stillness of the night Ruby can see the Milky Way glittering like a drift of diamonds cast over the deep black silk of the sky. From Fiddler's wood she hears the harsh cry of a vixen and she runs on, past Finch's farm and up towards the village.

In the vicarage garden, Ruby takes a handful of pebbles from her pocket and tosses them up against Davey's window. At the third attempt, the window swings open and Davey peers out. A minute later he has jumped down onto the grass beside her.

"You look like a brigand in that cloak," he says with a grin.

"Perhaps I am one," shrugs Ruby, turning away toward the gate.

Ruby leads the way to the old yew tree at the back of the churchyard. There, behind a crumbling tomb, the two of them made a den when they were children. The den has been cleared away long ago but the hidden hollow is still there.

"I found a poem on my dressing table," Ruby says, once they are sitting together, leaning their backs against the churchyard wall. "I've no idea how it could have got there."

"It must have been brought in by a bird ," says Davey. "The bird had very muddy feet."

"Do you like it?"

"I like it well enough." Ruby takes a sidelong look at Davey. "I thought perhaps you'd not want to know me once you got back from school, you being an educated gentleman now."

"I hated it there," says Davey. "I missed Bascome every day. "

"Are you back for good?"

Davey pauses. "My father insists that I go to Theological college. I have a scholarship starting in September."

Ruby's smile fades. "So you'll be a priest?"

"If I go."

"What else would you do?"

"I want to be a poet, but that's no way to make a living. Perhaps I'll be a farmer?"
"What do you know about that?"
"I could learn."
"I daresay you could try!" Ruby can't see Davey as a farmer.
Davey frowns and Ruby sees that she might have mocked him a little too much.
"I like your poems," she says. "Other people will too."
"My father would disown me if I refused to go to college, so I would need to learn some sort of trade. "
"You could be a school master. You were patient enough to teach me to read."
Davey looks at Ruby in surprise, remembering what happened when she asked him to teach her reading, the summer before he left for Bristol. "You didn't seem very keen at the time. You threw my English Grammar into the Folly Brook for being a load of contrary nonsense!"
"Did I do that?" Ruby laughs." Mostly I don't bother with it, but I can read well enough when I need to."
An easy silence grows between them and it is almost as if the last three years have not happened, as if they are still carefree children with the whole valley as their summer playground.

An unexpected grating noise rises against the stillness of the night; the sound of something heavy being dragged over rough stone. It's coming from somewhere nearby in the churchyard.

Ruby and Davey creep forward to peer round the trunk of the Yew tree. On the far side of the graveyard they see a man bending over one of the tombs. He has his back to them and holds a hooded lantern in his hand, its narrow beam illuminating the stonework of the tomb. Davey gasps in surprise as a bulky shape rises slowly from the ground at the man's feet.

The man with the lantern turns and glances nervously about. He is a scrawny fellow, dressed in a ragged velvet coat, his narrow face half hidden by a mess of dark hair. As he lifts the lantern and sweeps the beam of light over the gravestones, Ruby and Davey duck out of sight, but not before they have caught a glimpse of Mr Furey's ratty face.
"What's that maggot up to?" hisses Ruby.
Davey shrugs and they creep closer, taking care to stay well hidden.

Mr Furey sees nothing amiss in the shadows under the yew tree and turns back to the tomb. He reaches down to take the sack from his companion's outstretched hands and there is a dull clang as a spade is thrown up onto the grass. A large, pock marked face looms up and Captain Ransome climbs out to tower over Mr Furey like a weatherbeaten gargoyle. With a single heave of his strong arms, he slides the lid of the tomb closed.
"What do you think the Squire wants these old bones for?" asks Captain Ransome.
"Keep your voice down," hisses Mr Furey, glancing nervously over his shoulder. "The Squire pays us to do our job and keep our mouths shut."
"I know, but I just - " Captain Ransome is not a thoughtful man by nature but once he has an idea in his head he finds it hard to let it go.

"The Squire has other servants besides us. Very different kinds of servants, the sort that only come out at night - you know what I mean?"
Captain Ransome furrows his brow and looks troubled.
"Everybody has to eat, Ransome. I reckon if you carry on asking questions like that then we won't need to go digging in the graveyard to keep the Squire's pets happy - he'll just feed you to them instead."
Captain Ransome swallows hard.
"Alright, I just wondered . . ."
"Too much of that will get you killed," says Mr Furey. "Let's get this stuff back to the Hall."
Davey is watching the men with a wry grin on his face. He winks at Ruby and creeps forward to crouch behind a crumbling gravestone. He raises his hands to his mouth:
"Who's disturbin' my sleep?" he calls out in a wavering voice.
The two men freeze and stare about them in horror.
"Is that you, Jessie?" Davey continues. "I've been waitin' here for you in the cold earth all these years. Have you come to me at last? It's been so lonely without you . . ."
Mr Furey drops his sack and leaps away through the graveyard without a backward glance. Captain Ransome puts his hand on the hilt of his sword and scowls into the darkness, fear and suspicion struggling on his face. Davey lets out an eerie moan and the man's courage fails him. He turns tail and lumbers away after his companion, crashing off through the nettles to disappear around the side of

the church. Davey sinks to the ground, holding his sides in a fit of silent laughter, while Ruby crouches beside him, biting her knuckles to stop herself from laughing out loud.

When they go to investigate, they find the tomb shut fast. The sack that Mr Furey dropped lies in the nettles nearby. When Ruby lifts it open, a dusty human skull rolls out onto the ground.

"Troubling the living isn't enough for them," says Ruby grimly. "Now they want to turn the dead out of their homes as well."

"Grave robbing is a crime," says Davey. "We should tell someone."

"Who would we tell? Squire Colby is the Magistrate of Bascome valley and he won't be in a hurry to lock his own men up."

"Why would he want graveyard bones?"

There comes the sound of a door slamming and running feet on the cobbled street by the church. Leaving the bones where they are, Ruby and Davey slip away behind the Yew tree and over the wall.

Ruby is still pondering Davey's unanswered question as she makes her way home. She cannot fathom the purpose behind the grave robbing. She caught snatches of the whispered conversation between the Squire's henchmen but it made little sense - what kind of animal needs old bones to eat? The whole thing is very troubling. She wishes that there had been more time to talk with Davey. She wishes she could have told him what she is planning to do next but there is no way that she can share her secret - it is too dangerous; for Davey to know about Jack Shadow would make him an accomplice and he could hang for that.

Chapter 9.

Ruby is woken by the sound of Jet's barking. It is still dark and the chickens and geese are raising a terrible racket in the yard. The fox is back!

Ruby pulls on her boots and hurries down the stairs.

Seth is already awake and opening the back door. "See him off lad!" shouts Seth and Jet is out into the yard in a flash.

Ruby pushes past her father and peers out into the darkness. The hens are squawking madly and something large is thudding about inside the hen house. The door is off its hinges and the air is thick with feathers. Dark shapes move in the shadows of the chicken run. The creatures are too big to be foxes.

Jet runs to the edge of the chicken run and stops in his tracks. Something huge and dark leaps the fence and Jet sinks to the ground, whimpering. Ruby feels the hairs on her arms stand up. The creature is an enormous wolf with pitch black fur. The beast's shaggy shoulders stand as tall as Ruby's chest and its yellow eyes regard her with malevolent intelligence.

The wolf gives a snarl and leaps forward, knocking Jet onto his side and reaching for his throat with its teeth. Jet squirms and bites back madly at the wolf. He wriggles free but another lithe black shape leaps over the fence and falls on the helpless dog.

Ruby springs forward, picking up the axe from the chopping block and swinging it at the wolf that is pinning Jet down. The blow sends the wolf rolling back and Ruby swings the axe again, striking the second wolf on the shoulder. Jet shoots back into the house, yelping with terror. The wolves crouch back on their haunches, ready to spring, baring their teeth and snarling.

There is a crash of splintering wood and a flurry of darkness as two more of the beasts leap out, half destroying the hen house as they come. Ruby steps back to the door of the cottage with her axe held high. More shapes move in the shadows at the far side of the yard and three more wolves lope into view. The chickens and geese are all silent now - dead most likely.

"Get inside! " Ruby shouts to her father.

The advancing wolf pack pauses and the nearest beast sits back on its haunches. The slitted yellow eyes narrow and the creature draws back its lips, making a low growling, deep in its throat. It is not the noise of an animal; there are sounds inside the snarling like half formed words, deep and guttural. Ruby feels herself rooted to the spot with terror, her mind willing her to run, her body rigid with fear.

Behind Ruby, Seth has taken his rifle from the shelf over the mantelpiece and come to the doorway. He holds the gun in his arms, the barrel pointed at the ground.

"Out of the way girl," he shouts. "I can't see those beasts but I can hear them right enough. I'll soon send them packing."

When Ruby does not respond, Seth steps forward, blundering into her with his shoulder. The jolt breaks the enchantment and Ruby stumbles back to the safety of the doorway. As the wolf pack leap forward Seth raises the Flintlock and fires, aiming at the sound of running feet. The crashing blast of the rifle brings Ruby fully to her senses as the yard is lit up with orange fire from the muzzle flash. One of the wolves is thrown back against the wall of the barn and the others scatter. Ruby pushes Seth inside and bolts the door behind them.

They stand still in the dark house, hardly daring to breathe. There is no sound but the whimpering of Jet, curled up under Seth's chair. When Ruby cautiously opens the door again there is no sign of the wolves.
There is a clatter of feet on the stairs as Tom and Katy came down. When Tom hears that there are wolves about he is eager to be off after them.
"No lad," says Seth firmly. There is a sharp tone in his father's voice that Tom knows not to argue with.
Ruby lights the lantern while Katy fusses over Jet. He won't come out from under the chair and Katy cries when she sees that he is hurt.
"Sit in my chair," Seth says gently. "I'll soon put Jet right."
Seth coaxes the dog out but Jet whines as his fingers touch the gash in his flank.
"Tell me how he looks," Seth asks.
Tom brings the lantern and Ruby kneels on the floor in front of the whimpering dog. "His side has a long cut on it," she tells her father. "It isn't too bad, but the wound in his shoulder is deep."
Seth nods. He instructs Ruby which herbs to bring and sets to work making a poultice for Jet's shoulder. The dog lies still as Ruby and Seth sew closed the gash in his shoulder.

"He'll need to rest for a bit but he'll be right as rain in no time," says Seth.
Tom yawns and slouches back to bed, annoyed to have missed all the excitement. Katy's eyes are closing and Ruby takes her up the stairs but she is too rattled to go back to sleep herself.

"Those were no ordinary creatures," mutters Seth, as he sits down next to Ruby at the fireside. They have been out into the yard to see if any of the chickens or geese have survived but there are none left alive. "No beast I know of makes a sound like that. Nor gets up and walks away after it's been shot."
There should have been at least one dead wolf in the yard but there was nothing but a few scuffed paw prints. The dead chickens and Jet's bandaged shoulder are proof that the beasts were real but already the whole thing has the hazy feeling of a dream.
"I reckon we saw 'em off," Seth says softly, "but I won't be sleeping much tonight. Make the fire up, lass."
Seth leans forward to warm his hands at the embers and Ruby takes logs from the basket and blows on the coals until they flare up. The simple task of fire making steadies her nerves.
"What did the Squire want with you yesterday?" asks Seth, once the fire is blazing again.
"You don't miss much."
"Katy told me that he spoke to you. If Josia Colby is bothering you again then I'll go up to the Hall and speak to him. He's no right to do that."

"There's no need."

Seth is thoughtful. A log settles in the grate, sending a flurry of sparks up from the open stove to dance in the air like thistledown blown from a fiery flower. Ruby brushes a live ember from the hem of her dress before it can smoulder.

"You don't fancy going to live up at the Manor then?" Seth asks quietly.

Ruby narrows her eyes. "Don't even joke about that."

"I wouldn't blame you. You have a hard life here."

"Squire Colby makes my blood run cold. I'd rather die than . . ." She bites her lip. It was a stupid thing to say.

Ruby steals a glance at her father, his expression hasn't changed but she knows what he is thinking. They seldom speak about her mother; her death was so unexpected and so tragic for all of them. Ruby wishes that she could reach out to comfort her father but she can find no way to cross the distance that he keeps. All she can do is to look after the family as she promised. She will do it any way that she can, any way except one.

"The life I have here is all that I want," Ruby says.

Seth nods. "Josia Colby is as treacherous as winter and his heart is colder. Be careful of him."

"I will."

They sit in companionable silence while the fire burns down in the grate. After a while, Seth speaks again:

"Did you know that your grandmother was almost married to the Squire's father, Old Nathaniel Colby?"

Ruby looks up, astonished.

"Your grandma was the prettiest girl in Cornwall and Nathaniel Colby took quite a shine to her. He asked her to marry him but she refused, of course. He was as nasty a piece of work as his son is now. Nathaniel never got over it, they say, and he never married anyone else. That's why it was such a surprise when Josia showed up after the old Squire died."
"Do you think he really is Nathaniel's son?"
"There's no doubting it. There's a painting of Old Nathaniel Colby at the Hall and Josia is the spitting image of him."

Ruby looks up at the picture of her grandmother on the mantelpiece; a faded portrait in a tarnished silver frame, showing Lizzie Gilbert's mother, Catherine Sharpe. The glass is dusty and Ruby stands up to wipe it clean.
"You are very like her," Seth says.
Ruby can see that. The tall, dark haired woman in the picture smiles out at her with brown eyes that could be her own. It is curious to imagine how her life might have been if Catherine Sharpe had made a different choice and married the Squire's father instead of a farmer. Would Ruby have been born a lady up at the Manor? Perhaps she would not have been born at all?
"Catherine Sharpe had a lucky escape," says Ruby, putting her hand on her father's arm and yawning.

After Ruby has gone upstairs, Seth Gilbert sits alone in his chair by the fireplace. He keeps the loaded rifle over his knees, just in case the wolves come back. He listens to the sounds of the night but mostly he is thinking.

  When he and Tom ploughed up the blighted field that afternoon, they found the turnips and seed potatoes frozen solid. How could that happen in the middle of summer? Then there are the wolves; Seth picked up the dead chickens with his own hands. He did not see the creatures but the unearthly sound of the beast's voices still rings in his ears.

  Ruby sits on the edge of her bed, gazing out over the moonlit moor. The stars are bright and the night is still. Katy is breathing softly beside her. Are the dark wolves out there, running in the starlight? Ruby is too drowsy to give it any more thought. She kicks off her shoes and curls into bed, already half asleep. She does not see the shadow flitting over the window pane as the hawk takes wing and swoops down from the eaves. The empty eyed bird opens its beak and gives a harsh cry as it lifts away over Fiddler's wood and flies back up the valley.

Chapter 10.

In the still, silent hour before first cock crow, a black cloaked figure moves through Fiddler's Wood. There is no one to see Ruby slip along the path to the Tithe Cottages and no one to mark the rustle of grass as she steps back, a few moments later. A fox, slinking home along the Folly Brook, is the only one to notice. It is unusual to scent a human out so early and he pauses for a moment, his ears pricked, but all he hears is the wind in the leaves and the babble of the stream. With a shrug, the fox trots up the bank and ducks down under the fallen tree that hides the entrance to his den.

    Ruby runs up the lane and through the sleeping village. She has to reach Colby Hall before dawn; she needs a horse and it will be far easier to take one under cover of night. All the same, Ruby finds herself wishing that the sun would rise. She feels a new dread of the darkness, as if something were stalking her, skulking in the shadows at her back, waiting for right moment to pounce. She shakes off the memory of the wolves and their awful growling voices. She must have imagined that last part? Wolves do not speak. Things like that only happen in fairy tales. Besides, Seth chased the wolves off with his gun; they were beasts like any others.

    Ruby has three loaded pistols in the leather strap over her shoulder. She hopes that will be enough to see off anything she might meet.

A smudge of light glimmers on the Eastern horizon as she turns out of the lane to the Manor House. Colby Hall is silent, its edges blurred in the morning mist. Keeping to the trees, Ruby makes her way along the edge of the Manor grounds toward the stables. With any luck, the stable boys will still be asleep and she will able to sneak in and say hello to Caliban as she passes. Caliban's absence would be noticed at once during daylight but there are plenty of other horses at the Hall to choose from. It would be best to take one from the field by the edge of the wood. The fence there is old and it will be easy to make a hole in it. If anyone notices a horse missing then they will think it has escaped into the forest on its own.

The stallion raises his head and snorts a greeting when he sees Ruby at the door of his stall. She takes an apple from her pocket which he accepts graciously, allowing her to stroke his neck as he munches.

"I've not come to ride you," she whispers. "I'll take you out on the moors again soon."

She does not hate Caliban, despite what the stallion did to her father. As a child, Ruby often helped Seth in his work at the stables and she has ridden Caliban many times, though she was always careful not to let anyone see. Seth Gilbert loved the stallion's fiery spirit and he has passed that love on to his daughter.

There comes the sound of approaching footsteps from the yard and a peevish voice calls out:

"Stable boy! Are my horses ready?"

In a heartbeat, Ruby has jumped the door of Caliban's stall and hidden herself in the straw.

The footsteps come closer.

"I'm sure I heard someone in here," mutters the man. Ruby recognises the voice but she cannot not place it. The footsteps halt by the door of Caliban's stall.

Caliban clearly doesn't like the visitor. He puts his ears back, flares his nostrils and gives a whinny of annoyance. Working himself in a sudden fit of rage, he begins to turn about in his stall, snorting and stamping so wildly that Ruby has to scramble out of her hiding place to avoid being trampled. The stallion rears up and smashes his fore hooves into the stall door, shaking them almost off their hinges. Ruby presses herself up in the angle between the door post and the wall. She has never feared Caliban before, but now, trapped in the narrow stall as he rages and kicks, she is terrified. Caliban blinded her father. One stamp of those hooves could crush her skull like an egg.

The maddened stallion takes another wild turn about the stall, smashing the wooden manger to splinters as he goes. Ruby covers her face as fragments of wood rain down on her head. Caliban kicks out with his rear hooves at the wall and the whole barn trembles under the blow.

Ruby's hand goes to the chain at her neck, her fingers closing over the reassuring shape of the Kern.

Let Caliban be still. Let him be calm.

Almost at once, the stallion comes to a halt, standing in the centre of his stall and glaring malevolently at the man on the other side of the door. Ruby is amazed at the sudden change in Caliban. She has never thought of her mother's medallion as having any real power before. Perhaps there is something to the old tales after all?

Ruby edges her way along the door, keeping a wary eye on Caliban as she goes, and peeks out through a knot hole. She sees Mr Periwigge standing on the other side of the door, pale with shock.

More footsteps ring out and Mr Periwigge is joined by another man.

"Caliban is a mettlesome devil," says the Squire, clapping Mr Periwigge hard on the shoulder. "I've had a saddle on him myself but he wouldn't carry me. There's not a man I've met who can master him. Last year he all but killed my stableman." The Squire laughs." I shall breed from him, no doubt he'll sire a fine dynasty of racers."

Ruby bites back a snarl as she hears the Squire laughing at her father's fate. Her hand closes on the handle of her pistol and she imagines how it might feel to stand up and put a bullet through Josia Colby's heart. Her own heart beats faster at the thought of it but this is not the time to do anything foolish. She slides back over to the wall and forces herself to breathe slowly. Caliban shifts his weight from side to side and snorts contemptuously at the Squire.

"That horse, Josia," says Mr Periwigge, "I could swear that I have seen him before."

"I doubt it. There's not a beast to compare with him outside of the King's own stable. Caliban's sire belonged to the Sultan of Persia."

Mr Periwigge blinks and peers at the knife-shaped blaze of white on the stallion's forehead. "There is no mistaking it - this is the very beast ridden by the

highwayman who robbed me on the moors two nights ago."
"You're not a great expert on horseflesh, are you Charles?"
"Perhaps not," says Mr Periwigge, "but I know what I saw and I'm not likely to forget it. You just told me yourself that there's not another like him."
The Squire scowls and turns away.
"I need my horses in harness at once, Josia," says Mr Periwigge, turning to follow on the Squire's heels. "Where is your stableman?"

Ruby will have to move fast if she is to have any chance of getting out of the stable unseen. Once the men's footsteps have faded, she peers out over the top of the stall. Crossing the stable yard will be impossible now but there is a ladder leading up to the hayloft and a window at the other end of the loft that opens out to the forest.

Ruby jumps over the door of the stall and runs to the hayloft ladder. The window is unlocked and the shutter swings open easily. She hears raised voices in the stable yard and the sound of running feet. No time to lose!

The wall of the barn is too smooth to climb down but the ground at the bottom looks soft enough to jump. She climbs backwards out of the window, grabs the sill and lets herself down until she is hanging by her fingers. Then she lets go, remembering to bend her knees as she hits the ground. The breath is jolted out of her and she rolls sideways into a bed of nettles. She doesn't feel the pain of the stings on her hands until she is a hundred paces away, running through the trees.

She is pretty sure no one saw her but she will not risk taking any horses from the Hall today. There is no way to know if the Squire believes what Mr Periwigge has told him but if he does then it will be far more difficult to steal Caliban away in the future. There is no time to think about that now. Ruby will have to hurry if the rest of her plan is going to succeed.

Chapter 11.

The widow Marsh is still half asleep as she opens the back door of her cottage. Captain, her old black tomcat, gives a miaow of greeting and winds himself about her legs, purring. She bends down to scratch him behind the ear and he drops a dark bundle at her feet and looks up at her with his seagreen eyes.
"You old rascal," says widow Marsh affectionately. She makes to kick the dead bird away but it gives an unexpected clink as it rolls off the step. When she bends down to look more closely, widow Marsh finds that it is a small leather purse, heavy with coins.

 A little while later, Joe Temple goes to the well behind his cottage. The wooden bucket rattles against the stone rim of the well and as he reaches out to lift it free, he sees something shimmer in the water. Is it a fish? He looks more closely and sees that the bottom of the bucket is covered in bright silver coins.

 At the very same moment, at the end cottage, little Nelly Flynn is amazed at what she discovers in the grate when she goes to set the fire. She blinks and runs upstairs:
"Mam, Mam! The Fairies have been in the night and left gold in the hearth!"

 At midday, Mr Furey and Captain Ransome come calling at the Tithe Cottages. As they tie their horses to the fence by the sheep fold, Mr Furey notices smoke rising from the chimneys.
"Some people never learn," he mutters. "Ransome, go and tell them their time is up."

"We could have had 'em all out yesterday if we'd done it my way," says Captain Ransome, cracking his knuckles. "Just break their heads and chuck 'em out in the road."
"The Squire wants it done properly," says Mr Furey. "There's been trouble from that meddling lawyer in Truro and that little rabble rouser, Ruby Gilbert, was sticking her snout in yesterday. We're to give them one last chance to pay up an' then sling 'em out. You can break as many heads as you like after that."
The idea of inflicting violence upon his fellow man cheers Captain Ransome up no end.
"Let's start with the old Lady," he says.

When the two men knock on widow Marsh's door she answers with a smile and pays them the money that she owes in full. So do all the other tenants. Astonished, Mr Furey and Captain Ransome leave without a word.
"I'd like to know who gave those scum so much money," says Mr.Furey, as they untie their horses again.
"I'll leave it up to you to tell the Squire the good news," says Captain Ransome.
"Where are you off to?"
"There's that unfinished business from last night. You left the bag behind when you legged it - remember?"
"I didn't notice you hanging about," Mr Furey growls. "You ran even faster than me."
Captain Ransome reddens. "The Squire wants that stuff just as much as he wants them cottages emptied, so you do your job and I'll do mine, right?"

Mr Furey makes no reply. He doesn't fancy going back to the churchyard, even by daylight.

Mr Furey rides slowly back toward the Manor House. He is not looking forward to telling the Squire that the Tithe cottages are still tenanted but he has other things on his mind by the time he reaches Colby Hall:

At the end of Sharrow Lane, Mr Furey jumps down to unlatch the gate. When he turns back to his horse, he finds himself facing a tall figure in a black cloak. A black scarf hides the stranger's face and a wide brimmed hat is pulled down low over the eyes. The stranger's gloved hands hold a pistol which is pointed straight at Mr Furey's heart.

"Don't murder me!" cries Mr Furey, before the highwayman can utter a word. If Mr Furey had been a little less terrified then he might have noticed that the highwayman is standing on a tree stump, half hidden by the hem of the black cloak.

"If you give me no cause to shoot, then I shall let you live. I've no wish to waste my powder on a rat like you." The highwayman's shadowed eyes flash dangerously. "You've been collecting the rents I believe?"

Mr Furey swallows hard and nods.

"Are the takings in the saddle bags?"

Mr Furey nods again. The Squire's money is not worth dying for.

The highwayman gestures with the pistol: "Lie down on the road."

Once Mr Furey is face down in the mud, the masked figure jumps down from the tree stump and steps to the side of the horse. A quick rummage in the saddle bags and the rent money is found. The highwayman puts the bag of coins into the folds of the cloak, slips a foot into the stirrup and leaps up onto Mr Furey's horse.

"Get up now," the highwayman says wheeling the horse around.

The terrified Mr Furey rises to his feet and looks up at the rider.

"Get back to Josia Colby," says the highwayman, "and tell him that Jack Shadow sends his compliments."

Mr Furey takes to his heels and does not stop running until he has reached the Manor house.

"So much for a lesson in respect," Ruby smiles to herself as she watches Mr Furey's retreating back. She is still smiling as she rides away, but her sense of triumph is short lived.

At the corner of Sharrow Lane, Ruby comes face to face with a company of soldiers; a column of twenty men on foot and two officers on horseback. They wear long red coats and the foot soldiers carry muskets over their shoulders.

Ruby's heart misses a beat as she reins in her horse and freezes in the middle of the road. The soldiers halt too, as surprised as she is; they had not expected to come face to face with Jack Shadow in broad daylight, at the very gates of Colby Hall. There is stunned silence as the Captain of the troopers sits open mouthed on his horse, blinking at the masked rider.

Ruby whirls her horse about and gallops away. "Halt - In the name of the king!" shouts the Captain. Ruby has no intention of waiting around for anyone - not even the king - and she speeds back up the lane without a backward glance. Dimly, she hears the Captain give the order to shoot and hears the crack of musket fire behind her. A bullet whistles past her ear as she turns the corner and then she is safe - for a moment at least - out of sight behind the trees. She turns her horse into the wood, ducking down in the saddle to avoid the low branches. The Captain and his Lieutenant spur their own horses forward, sending the foot soldiers scattering into the hedge. They turn the corner just in time to see Ruby disappearing into the trees.

Ruby knows the ground better than her pursuers and the stolen horse is small and nimble. She finds a narrow track through the wood and pushes the young filly on as hard as she dares, leaping fallen trees and riding breathlessly close to the overhanging branches. She is just starting to put real distance between herself and the soldiers when the track widens out into a leafy lane. The soldiers will have the edge on Ruby here. Her horse is eager but it is no match for the thoroughbreds that the officers ride. Ruby wishes with all her heart that she were riding Caliban.

The thorny hedges to either side of the lane are too thick to ride through and there is no time to double back. No choice but to ride on down the middle of the

open road. Shooting from the back of a galloping horse is not easy but the men behind her are trained soldiers. Ruby's only chance is to reach the bottom of the hill as fast as she can. The lane twists and turns there, giving her better cover from the soldier's pistols.
Ruby leans close to the horse's neck.
"Run girl - run as fast as you can!"
The little horse gives a snort and a sudden burst of speed, scattering pebbles from her hooves. There are shouts as the soldiers gallop into the lane and Ruby hears the crack of a pistol. The shot goes wide and the soldiers spur their horses on, preferring to run their quarry down rather than waste more powder.

   Ruby has a good lead on her pursuers but it is shrinking as the lane dips down the hill. The road sinks between high banks, lined with mossy stones. There are two quick bends and then Ruby sees the tree. It is a tall oak with its branches hanging over the lane. She knows at once what she must do. It is plain crazy, and likely to get her killed, but she is desperate. Her little horse is already tiring and it is a mile until the nearest gate and any hope of an escape route. The soldiers will catch her long before then.

   She shakes her feet free of the stirrups and lifts herself to crouch on the saddle, gripping onto the pommel with both hands to steady herself. It feels as if she going to tumble off at any second but there is no time to be afraid. The branch rushes towards her and she jumps, catching hold of it in her gloved hands. Her momentum swings her body forward and the branch bends to take the strain. At the far end of the swing, she twists, lets go of the branch and flies up over hedge. For one heart stopping moment, Ruby is weightless, sailing up into a dazzling blur of light and leaf shadows, then she crashes onto the ground on the far side, hitting the earth hard and rolling into a drift of dry leaves.

The riderless horse goes swifter now and it has galloped out of sight around the next bend before the soldiers turn the corner by the tree. They speed on, following the sound of hoofbeats, never suspecting that Ruby has jumped free.

Ruby lies stunned on the ground beside the hedge, breathless and amazed that her plan has worked. She has practiced trick riding before, standing up on the back of a pony for a few steps and jumping off, but she has only ever done it at a slow trot and there was always been plenty of soft heather to break her fall. Leaping from a galloping horse was insanely risky but it was exhilarating!

Things haven't gone quite as Ruby planned so far this morning but she has saved the tenants of the Tithe cottages from eviction and stolen back the money into the bargain. She is covered in bruises but she is alive.

She listens to the fading sound of the soldier's horses. When she is sure that they are gone, Ruby climbs to her feet, picks up her hat, and creeps back along the hedge.

It is a nerve wracking business going through the wood. The rest of the soldiers come running past along the road but they make such a racket that Ruby has plenty of time to hide. Ruby knows how to move quietly and she soon finds the place where she hid her washing basket. She transforms herself from a desperate highwayman into an innocent looking farmer's daughter and puts the pistols, hat and cloak, at the bottom of the basket, along with the rent money, all covered over with a layer of clean washing.

  The woods are quiet and the village too, until Ruby turns the corner at the bottom of the hill. There are at least twenty horses tied up outside the Inn and more of them grazing along the bank of the river. The White Horse is full to bursting and the drinkers have spilled out on to the cobbles outside. Most of the men are troopers. A large group sit around a table by the door with wooden flagons of cider set before them.
  Ruby puts her head down and quickens her pace. The troopers see a village girl with a basket, not a dangerous outlaw. Heart in her mouth, she crosses the bridge and heads up the lane. At the first gate she cuts through and crosses a field to pick up the overgrown path up to Fiddler's wood.

Chapter 12.

Davey is turning the handle of the front door when he hears his father's voice behind him:
"Where do you think you are you going?"
Davey turns to meet the Reverend Tachard's severe gaze. The Reverend is a tall, thin man, with a wild mane of white hair and a sharp, bird-like face that seems permanently drawn into an expression of displeasure. Davey's mother stands beside him, small and mousey next to her overbearing husband.
"I am taking my books up to the wood to study, father."
"Don't lie to me!" snaps the Reverend Tachard. He strides forward and snatches the book out of Davey's hand.
"What is this nonsense?" He scowls at the title on the spine. "Paradise Lost? You should be reading the scriptures not idling your time away with poetry."
The Reverend thumps the book against the banister and glares at Davey. "You waste your days scribbling verse and gadding about with that wayward Gilbert girl while your school books go untouched."
Davey thinks of the pile of theological texts gathering dust on his desk. He has tried to read them many times but each time he does he feels his eyelids drooping. Now he is free from school he would much rather be out on the moors or walking through the woods.
"There's plenty of time before I go back to school -"
The Reverend takes a step closer and jabs his bony finger into Davey's chest. "You are not a child any

more. I expect you to apply yourself to your studies at home from now on. You will certainly not be going to Truro on market day. Your mother will not hear of it, not with that highwayman about."

"Jack Shadow wouldn't stop a farmer's cart."

"The man is a dangerous criminal! I daresay there are plenty of ignorant folk who admire scoundrels like Midnight Jack, or whatever he is called, but he is no hero. People would do better to seek God's Grace than put faith in a brigand. Until the highwayman is apprehended, you will not go to Truro - that is the end of it."

Davey holds his father's gaze. He has no intention of staying at home on market day but there is no point in arguing; the old man is too set in his ways.

"You should make an effort to seek out the company of your equals," the Reverend Tachard continues. "Squire Colby is a man of good breeding and I feel sure that if you present yourself to him at the Manor House he could find you some useful employment -"

"Squire Colby is no gentleman!" says Davey. "Do you think that the way that he turns honest folks out of their homes to starve is Christian? He would like nothing better than to dig up the whole valley and turn it into a smoking tin mine -"

"You will not interrupt me while I am speaking!" snarls the Reverend, his face reddening with rage. "The squire has influence with the Bishop, which could help you greatly once you have completed your studies. As to his business ventures, they are not our concern. He is very generous to the church -"

"You hypocrite!"

"Enough!" the Reverend slaps Davey hard across the face and Davey falls back against the wall, sending a shudder through the little house that sets the china plates rattling in the dining room cabinet. "You will do as I tell you. There will be no more poetry and no more insolence. You are not too old for a thrashing!" The blow took Davey by surprise but his father's threats don't frighten him the way they used to. Davey has grown taller in the last year and he has learned more than Latin and Greek in his time away at school. As the Reverend Tachard raises his fist a second time Davey grabs his father's arm and holds it. He glares back at his father and for a brief, rage-filled instant Davey can think of nothing but repaying his father for every blow that he has ever given him.

Davey throws aside his father's arm and steps forward. The Reverend Tachard falls back, bewildered but as Davey looks into his father's eyes he sees, not the fearsome bully of his childhood, but a lost and frightened old man. He notices the pleading look on his mother's face, puts down his fists and steps back:

"I apologise if I spoke out of turn, father," says Davey. "I will return to my studies later."

He takes the book of poetry from his father's hand and turns for the door.

Once the front door has slammed behind him Davey is free. There will be more arguments later but his father will not make a scene in the street; he is too concerned about his reputation for that.

Davey breaks into a run, his rage at his father driving him forward. He passes the churchyard, the forge and the White Horse Inn, where soldiers sit with their cider. He hardly notices them. He runs over the bridge and along the lane, vaults a gate and runs on through the long grass. He runs until his rage is gone and then he throws himself down on the ground to get his breath back.

Davey sits up. His lip is bleeding. His cheek does not hurt much but a dull ache has lodged itself somewhere near his heart. He shivers, overtaken by a sudden loneliness. He is glad that he stood up to his father but something has broken inside him. The feeling is not a comfortable one but there is truth in it. One thing is certain; Davey will never let the Reverend Tachard tell him what to do ever again.

Davey turns as he hears the swishing sound of someone approaching through the long grass. He jumps up and comes face to face with Ruby, hurrying home with her basket on her hip.
"It's alright for some," laughs Ruby, "sleeping the morning away while the rest of us have to work -" She notices Davey's split lip and stops." Oh! What happened? Did you run into Captain Ransom again?"
"My father and I had an argument," says Davey. He shrugs and gives a tight smile. "It's nothing."
"He hit you?"
"My father thinks that I am not spending enough time studying. He is right, of course, but I have no intention of changing my ways." Davey smiles. It is a real smile this time, with a twinkle in it. "I was down by the inn yesterday and Tad Willow told me a fine tale. Do you want to hear it?"

"Tell it as we walk," says Ruby. "I need to get these things home." She would like nothing better than to sped the day with Davey, sitting by the stream, telling stories, but she won't feel safe until she has hidden her pistols and the stolen money.

Davey falls in step beside Ruby and they head up the path toward the wood.

"Tad said that the wolves have returned to Cornwall," says Davey. "They came back last winter, after Squire Colby opened his mine up by Axe Tor. Tad says that the wolves were sleeping under the earth and all the digging woke them up. They are no ordinary beasts. They are Witch Wolves, with eyes like lanterns and coats black as pitch. They are too clever to fall into any trap and they can't be killed with a gun or a spear.

"The Queen of Faerie made them, long ago. She wanted fierce servants to guard her palace so she took the souls of men and put them into the bodies of wolves. But the men's souls became angry with their lot. They rebelled against the Queen and she had them imprisoned in the earth. They would have slept there until Judgement Day if the mine hadn't been dug and disturbed their slumber. The Witch Wolves are filled with hatred for all living things - especially humans, for seeing us reminds them of what they have lost.

The wolves come in the night to lonely farms and steal children away so that they can suckle on their blood. The infants are found the next morning, pale and cold, sometimes alive, sometimes dead . . "

Davey stops. He turns to look at Ruby, who has halted in her tracks. He sees the stricken look on her face.

"What's wrong? It's only one of Tad's stories."

"It's no story, Davey. Those wolves came to our cottage last night."

"You've seen them? It doesn't seem possible."

"I saw the wolves with my own eyes. And I've heard a legend like that before."

"Where did you hear it?"

It was in the little book that Jack Shadow stole from Mr Periwigge but Ruby can't tell Davey about that. "My father is like old Tad," she says quickly." He tells all sorts of stories." Ruby hates the easy way the lie comes but it is too dangerous to trust anyone. So much has happened since yesterday and she needs time to think. "I'd like to stay and talk, Davey, but I have a lot to do today."

"I'll come with you to the top of the hill," says Davey. "Let me take the basket for a bit. It looks heavy."

Before Ruby knows it, Davey has taken the basket. She hears the clink of coins and sees the bemused look on Davey's face.

"What have you got under your laundry?" asks Davey. "This weighs a ton."

"Just some old pots I took to be mended at the forge," says Ruby, "and I'm quite capable of carrying it myself." She puts out her arms and Davey hands the basket back. She turns away again up the path and Davey stands looking after her. What has he done to upset her?

"Are you still coming to Truro tomorrow?" he calls. "Farmer Finch is setting off just after sunrise."
"I'll meet you at the bottom of Gilbert's lane," Ruby says, flashing a smile back at Davey.

Ruby walks on in a daze. She hates lying to Davey and now she's hurt his feelings into the bargain. Each lie she tells seems to lead to another, trapping her in a web of her own making. The situation is becoming more perilous by the hour. It was a close run thing with the troopers on Sharrow Lane and at the stables first thing this morning. There are soldiers everywhere now. Perhaps it is time for Jack Shadow to disappear? The tenants of the Tithe cottages are safe and if she can sell the snuffbox and ring she will have enough money to see her family through the winter.

Only one thing makes Ruby pause: with Jack Shadow gone, who will be left to stand against the Squire and his men?

Ruby stops at the door of the barn. At the far end of the field Seth and Tom are ploughing with Bessie, while Katy rides on the old carthorse's back, laughing and chattering happily. Ruby slips into the barn and goes to the place at the back where the empty apple boxes are stacked. She sweeps the straw aside with her hands and lifts up the loose board. It's not safe to hide things so near the house. She'll have to move everything to the hollow tree as soon as she gets a chance.

She lifts aside Mr Periwigge's silver pistol and takes The Keys of Queen Mab out from her hidey hole. She leafs through the pages until she finds the part that she began reading the other day by the folly brook:

" They are seven in number and they resemble wolves, though they are larger than any mortal wolf and their coats are dark as sunless night. These creatures were once men and they retain the souls and wits of men and have a speech all of their own that is awful to hear.

The Witch Wolves must be summoned in darkness and, once called, they may only remain in the waking world for the span of a single night. The summoning is perilous and the cost of the charm is steep. Rare spices must be burned, pledges made to the dark powers, and the beasts must eat of the bones of the long dead, freshly dug from the earth. The summoner must let the creatures lap at his own life's blood in order to bind them to his will."

There follows what looks like a spell, written in a language that Ruby cannot understand. The book is not a collection of fairy tales - it is a book of magic!

There is evil at work in Bascome valley, something that reaches far beyond Squire Colby's ruthless greed for land and money. Ruby has no name for it yet but she has no doubt that its heart lies at Colby Hall; she must go there tonight, before the troopers make things too difficult - she has to find out more.

Chapter 13.

The crumbling walls of the East Wing of Colby Hall are thick with ivy and the trees grow so near the house here that it is an easy matter to creep close without being seen. The derelict part of the house will be the best way in. From here, Ruby can make her way to the more inhabited regions and begin her search. She has no clear idea what she is looking for but she guesses that she will know it when she finds it.

   The moon is hidden behind the clouds and it is pitch dark under the trees. Ruby creeps slowly forward, searching for a way in. As she makes her way along the side of the house, Ruby becomes aware of a hollow drumming sound from inside, like the pounding of running feet on floorboards. Could the troopers be here? Have they been watching her from the upper windows? The sound is getting louder. Ruby steps into the cover of the ivy and pulls a pistol from her belt.

   The running feet come closer still. The rhythm of the noise is more like the galloping of horses that the tread of men's feet. There is a scrabbling sound and a dark shape leaps from the window only a few feet ahead of her. A wolf! It is huge and jet black, with sharp white teeth and eyes like yellow flames. There is no doubt now - they are real!

   Ruby cowers back as, one after another, all seven of the Witch Wolves jump from the window and bound away into the forest. They move with terrible purpose, oblivious to Ruby as she presses herself back into the shadows, breathless with terror.

There is no Spell of Forgetting to cloud Ruby's mind this time and it is a long while before she dares to move. Only when she is certain that the wolves are long gone does she set off again. There is no doubt where she must go; in through the window that the wolves leapt out from.

The glass is long gone from the window and the wooden frame is soft with rot. The room inside is filled with mouldering furniture and leaves lie thick underfoot. Pale toadstools grow in the damp corners and there are sycamore seedlings pushing up through the floorboards by the window. Ruby jumps over the sill and makes her way into the dark interior. The door of the rotting room opens onto a corridor ankle deep with dry leaves. Large chunks of plaster have fallen from the ceiling and the prints of the wolves' paws are plain to see in the dust.

Ruby follows the wolf tracks.

The leaf-filled corridor leads deeper into the dark interior of the hall. Ruby is forced to go slowly, pausing to search for wolf prints, feeling her way on her hands and knees in the dimmest places. She has just reached a tiled hallway at the foot of a wide stair when she sees the yellow glow of a lantern, moving unsteadily over the peeling wallpaper of the gallery above. Ruby steps out of sight behind a door and waits.

A figure appears on the landing. A large man in a cloak and hood. He is bent forward, his shadow looming over the wall like the silhouette of a stooping giant. Ruby takes the man for a hunchback, until she sees the heavy bundle carried over his shoulder. The hooded man pauses at the head of the stairs to adjust his burden, then begins to descend, one step at a time.

It is only as he passes the doorway where Ruby crouches that she sees that the man is carrying the body of a girl, her arms hanging limp down his back. Ruby stifles a cry as she sees the girl's pale face, her wide unseeing eyes and lolling tongue.

Once the light has faded, Ruby steps out from her hiding place and follows, letting the glimmer of the lantern on the walls ahead guide her.

The hooded man takes several turns before pausing at a heavy oak door. He places his lantern on an iron hook and takes a key from the folds of his black robe. He unlocks the door, lifts the lantern again and steps through, leaving the door unlocked behind him. Ruby follows. Stone steps wind down into darkness. The stairs are ancient, the stones worn away by the passage of countless feet. There are stories that Colby Hall was built on the foundations of a much older castle. The worn stair must lead down to the castle cellars.

Ruby hears the rattle of a key in the darkness below and creeps down the stairs as quickly as she dares. At the bottom is a low corridor. Lamplight spills from an open doorway ahead of her. Ruby moves softly to the doorway and inches her head around the frame.

The hooded man stands in the middle of the cell, the body of the dead servant girl lying on the floor at at his feet. He turns her over with his foot and stares down at her.

"You were hardly ideal material," he mutters. "A waste of time giving you the potion."

The man straightens and turns away. Ruby jumps back out of sight just in time, her heart thumping. There comes a sound from somewhere in the dark, a low moan from further down the corridor.

Ruby runs back, silent and swift, up the stone stair, and retraces her steps to the gallery. She climbs the staircase and makes for the doorway that the hooded man first emerged from. There are wolf prints here, underneath the dragging foot marks. She follows the trail, past shadowed doorways, rotting tapestries and faded portraits of forgotten Colby ancestors. She climbs the twisting tower stair and reaches the door at the top. Finding the door unlocked, Ruby steps inside.

The room is silent, save for the ticking of a clock. A long table runs the length of the chamber toward the window at the far end, where a patch of moonlight falls. There are pale shapes on the table that look like the bones of animals.

The objects at the far end of the table are illuminated more clearly: a silver bowl, a knife with a carved handle and a pile of leather bound books. Ruby traces a gloved forefinger along the spines of the books: The Book of Malachai the Necromancer, the Secrets of the Viper's Tongue, Corpus Maleficium. A fourth book lies open on the table. Its heavy pages are blank but between them lie tattered scraps of paper, the carefully preserved remains of a far older book. The pages of this book have been badly burned but Ruby recognises pages from The Keys of Queen Mab.

The text of the left hand page is the very same that Ruby read in the barn, dealing with the summoning of Mab's Hounds, but the right hand page is from another part of the book:

"A magician may make his own servants in the manner of Mab's Hounds but their powers will be less - according to the skill of the one who creates them. A willing soul makes the most obedient servant, though the transformation may equally be forced upon the unwilling. The creature made will remain as a beast between dusk and dawn and at sunrise return to his human form, oftentimes with no memory of the change.

A potion must be made and the ingredients steeped in the subject's own blood by the light of the full moon."

The paper has been badly burned and the method of making the potion is hard to read. Ruby slips off her glove and turns the page. The borders of this section are illustrated with a smoke of swirling eyes, claws and half formed faces.

"The devouring spirits of Blight and Famine require payment to serve. Hemlock, viper's tongue, rust from a coffin nail and graveyard bones must be burned. The ruinous spirits may then be summoned from the smoke and sent forth upon the magician's bidding.

Their touch withers all living plants, turns wood to rot and sours fresh water. If they be sent to plague a man or animal they may sap his life until he die."

In a trance of horror, Ruby turns the page. The next section has been taken from a different part of the book and the scorched pages are decorated with drawings of twisting snakes.

"There is an elixir that may be drunk by a mortal man that, no matter how old or sick he be, he shall be returned into the strength of his youth. If the enchantment is successful, the magician will fall into the semblance of death. Though he seem dead, he shall not die, but awaken, rejuvenated.

The elixir does not give the true immortality of the Fairie Folk, but a man may live for many hundreds of years this way.

For the making of the elixir:

An ounce of cinnabar, ground and mixed with quicksilver; sap from the yew tree; the tears of an adder; the blood of a child less than one year old, caught in the shell of a salamanders egg."

Ruby has heard whispered stories about the old Squire being a sorcerer but she had never thought them anything but tall tales. Could they be true, after all?

" There is only one way that a man may attain the true immortality; If he seek the jewel known as the

Faerie Star and dare to wield it against Queen Mab herself -"

She is startled by a footfall on the stair. She forgets the book and looks wildly about her; aside from the patch of moonlight, the room is in complete darkness. There might be a hundred hiding places - or none. Even if she could find somewhere to hide, Ruby does not wish to stay for another moment in this deathly place. She turns to the window and pushes it open.

The wall falls sheer down to the trees, a hundred feet below. The stones are rough, with plenty of handholds and there is a dense growth of ivy but there is no way that Ruby can climb down unseen from the window - the moon is out now, lighting up the scene as clear as day. She glances upwards to see thick ivy running to the roof of the tower.

The footsteps have halted on the landing and a line of yellow lamplight shines at the crack below the door. The doorknob turns.

Tearing her eyes away from the dizzying drop, Ruby hauls herself onto the window sill, takes hold of a thick ivy stem and begins to climb. The stem snaps as soon as she puts her whole weight on it and she falls back, her mouth stretching open in a silent scream. She reaches out with her hands and slides painfully down the stone wall, groping wildly for a handhold. She catches another ivy stem and her foot finds a gap in the stones. The stem holds and she braces herself against the wall, her heart racing.

She forces herself to look up. Beside the window there is a gap between the ivy and the wall. The space is filled with dry leaves and old birds nests but there is room to for her inside. She hauls herself up and wriggles into the gap, holding onto the rough ivy stems for dear life. She has to pray that she has not been heard.

The ivy stems bite into the palm of her ungloved right hand. Her glove - she left it on the table! She turns toward the window. Lamplight moves on the wall of the room. There is no time to go back.

Lamplight flares on the leaded glass. The footsteps halt and the dark bulk of a hooded man's head and shoulders are thrust suddenly out of the window. The man looks down the ivy covered wall, his face hidden in the cowl of his hood, His hands grip the stone sill, only inches from Ruby's face. He is so close that Ruby can hear the rasp of his breath and see the soot stains on his finger tips.

"Where are you?" he hisses. "Running from me like a thief in the night?"

Ruby's heart jumps. Has he seen her?

The man remains as he was, staring out into the forest.

"You must be near," he whispers. "But you had time enough to make your escape." The man laughs.

He has no idea that she is there but at any moment he might turn and see her.

"Jack Shadow! Until now you have left no trace upon the world but the rumour of your name."

The man lifts his right hand and there is something dark clenched between his fingers - Ruby's glove!

"I have you now. Once my wolves have returned from the moors, I will set them on your trail."

Ruby holds her breath and does all she can to imagine herself invisible. Her mouth and nose are filled with leaf dust from her fall through the ivy and, to her horror, she feels the first itch of a sneeze. She wills it away, biting her lip hard and fixing her eyes on the man's hands. They are the hands of a gentleman, the fingernails unbroken and neatly trimmed. On the left hand is a silver ring set with a green stone. She knows that ring. She saw it only two days before as the Squire had tried to run her into the hedge with his horse. Squire Colby!

Every sinew of Ruby's body is stretched as tight a bow string. All it would take is a single turn of his head; the moonlight is horribly bright and there has been no time to pull the scarf over her face - the Squire would know her at once.

Squire Colby leans forward and swings his gaze over the wall but he does not turn far enough to see Ruby.

"There will be reckoning, Jack Shadow," he mutters. "And I will have back what you stole from me."

He turns away and closes the window behind him.

Ruby breathes deeply and slides her left foot slowly over to a thick ivy stem. She rests her weight and relieves her aching arms. She can hear the floorboards creak as the Squire moves about inside the room.

A breeze gusts up, ruffling the leaves, and Ruby takes the opportunity to begin climbing, slow and stealthy, down the ivy covered wall of the tower.

By the time Ruby reaches the ground her arms and legs are like jelly. She stumbles a few steps into trees and falls to the ground, her breath coming in deep gasps. She feels the cool wetness of damp leaves on her face, drinks in the scent of the earth and listens to the thudding of her heart as it gradually slows. She recalls the sight of the pale girl lying dead on the floor of the dungeon and shudders - it might so easily have been her.

Fear makes Ruby's mind as sharp as a knife. She has to get rid of her remaining glove and find a way of putting the wolves off her scent. She gets to her feet and sets off through the trees, running uphill, heading deeper into the forest.

A mile above the hall, she finds a stream. She throws her glove into the bushes on the far side, steps into the water and wades to the middle. She makes her way downstream, keeping well away from the banks, wading in the shallower places, scrambling over waterfalls and swimming through the deep pools. Staying in the water is her only hope. It will mask her scent and throw the wolves off her trail. She is glad of the cold. It keeps her senses sharp.

The stream bed is slippery and Ruby loses count of the number of times she falls. She is bruised all over and covered from head to toe in mud and rotten leaves. Her boots are full of water and the powder in her pistol is soaked. She presses on, too intent on keeping her footing to waste time looking over her shoulder.

At last, she comes to a place that she knows, where willow trees grow thick along the banks of the stream.

She pulls herself up onto an overhanging branch and creeps along it, past the trunk and on into the next tree. She goes as far as she can this way, branch to branch and tree to tree, until the willows thin out. At the edge of the willows she jumps to the ground and runs back through the woods toward Bascome.

Ruby pauses by the vicarage. She is tired, frightened and alone. She wants, more than anything, to talk to Davey about what she has discovered. She needn't tell him about Jack Shadow, but the Squire must be stopped somehow. She cannot do it alone.

The Squire is a sorcerer. That seems clear enough. Ruby has never believed in such things, except in stories, but she has seen the Witch Wolves with her own eyes and she has felt the power of their voices. She has seen the Keys of Queen Mab and the room in the ivy covered tower. Does the Squire really have the power to wield dark magic? She remembers the eyeless hawk and the terror that it brought. She remembers the withered field. These things cannot be explained away. She knows, deep in her bones, that she has stumbled on the truth about Squire Colby.

She needs to get warm and dry. She needs to sleep before she can begin to make any sort of a plan.

Chapter 14.

He has set a bowl of water on the table by the window. From an ebony box at his side he takes a pinch of silvery dust. He sprinkles the dust onto the water and begins to chant.

"Moth and Moonstone, Willow dew
Owl's eye, Silver, sap of Yew
Open Moon Mirror - Show me True."

The grains of dust shimmer as they dissolve. The glimmer fades and the surface of the water is silvered and smooth as glass.
The Witch Wolves have failed to discover Jack Shadow's scent but there are other ways to find him. He takes the strand of horse hair that he found snagged in the seam of the black glove and drops it into the bowl. The hair floats for a moment, the mirrored surface warping to buoy it up, then sinks to the bottom of the bowl. He closes his eyes and takes a deep breath.
"Show me the one who comes to my stables and steals Caliban away," he says.
He gazes down at the Moonmirror. At first he sees nothing but the moon herself glimmering like a bright coin. Clouds swirl and clear to reveal the image of a black horse with a white blaze upon its nose. The horse has sacking tied around its hooves and it is being led into a stable by a figure wrapped in a black cloak. Josia Colby leans closer, trying to see the face of the figure holding the reins. The cloaked man's hat

is pulled down over his eyes and his features are hidden. The Squire mutters under his breath:
"Show me clearer."
The image in the mirror dissolves and another comes. The horse is gone and the cloaked figure is walking through a misty wood. A house appears in the fog; Gilbert's cottage. The Squire leans closer, trying to glimpse the man's face but in his eagerness the sleeve of his robe sweeps across the bowl and the image fades, leaving only clear water.
"I have you now!"

In the dungeon, far below the tower, Lucy Cotton lies on the stone floor, her soul balanced on the very edge of death. She lies unmoving for many hours, poison choking at her heart, her breath no more than a whisper. She drifts into darkness, her memories falling away. The spells work their changes, unraveling and reshaping the weave of her bones.

After a measureless time, she wakes.

When she opens her eyes, she finds her senses sharp and her body strong. The ropes that bound her have fallen away and she gets to her feet and stretches. From the crack under the dungeon door blows a trickle of stale air. She pushes her shoulder against the door but it is locked fast. She circles the cell, searching for a way out. From the far corner comes a faint breeze. The air smells cool and fresh. She pushes at the stones until she finds a loose one. She pulls and scratches until the stone falls free and the breeze grows stronger. She pulls at another stone, then another. Earth falls around her as she digs. Then there comes a shudder and a rumble. Stone grates on stone and the wall collapses with a crash. The ceiling caves in and she is borne down beneath an avalanche of earth.

Earth fills her eyes and mouth. She tastes the earth on her tongue and is seized by blind terror. She strains her body against the deadly weight and begins to move, wriggling forward, painfully slowly, through the earth fall. Her breath burns in her lungs and the blood thunders in her ears. She feels her limbs begin to weaken but she presses on.

At last, an agonising thrust of her body brings her mouth out into the air. She coughs up mud and bile and takes a gulping breath. She drinks in the sweet night air and when she is rested enough she begins to twist herself free. She tumbles out onto the ground and lies panting in the moonlight.

The night breeze is soft. She can smell wild roses and honeysuckle, leaf mould, dew and moonlight. She has never known moonlight to have a smell before but it does not seem strange to her. The scent is clear and cool and full of music and the full moon shines down as brightly as the sun. She shakes herself, blinks the earth from her eyes and scrambles away into the tress. Her feet are sure and swift and her heart is full of joy as she runs.

Chapter 15.

Davey lets himself out of his bedroom window and makes his way carefully along the ridge of the roof below. The sun has just risen and the land all about is wrapped in a fine mist. The rooftops of the village snake off ahead of him in the yellow dawn, each one a little lower than the last, descending the hillside like steps. Ruby once challenged him to go the length of the village along the rooftops, right down to the inn. They were nine years old then and it had been a great adventure but this morning the dew makes the slate roofs slippery and Davey decides not to risk his neck. He slides down from the roof onto the garden wall, jumps onto the cobbles and sets off down the street.

  At Finch's Farm, Davey is greeted with a friendly nod and sets to helping Farmer Finch lift baskets of vegetables onto the back of the cart. When the wagon is loaded Mrs Finch waves them off from the farmhouse door and they head off down the valley.

  Ruby stands waiting at the bottom of Gilbert's lane, a bundle slung over her shoulder. She greets Davey with a grin and jumps up next to him on the seat of the cart. The mist is already clearing and the sun slanting through the high hedge to warm their faces. It promises be a fine day
"Your father changed his mind then?" says Finch to Davey, after a while." I had word you wasn't coming along today."

Sam Finch is well built, with a broad face burned brown from the sun. He smiles easily and his blue eyes twinkle with mischief.

"I changed it back for him," says Davey.

Farmer Finch takes a sidelong glance at Ruby and Davey sitting beside him on the wide driving seat. "I wonder why?"

Davey pretends not to notice.

"And you're not worried about highwaymen Ruby?" asks Sam, when he sees that Davey is not going to rise to his teasing.

Ruby is only half listening. She is thinking about what she will say to Davey, as soon as she gets the chance, and how she can tell him what she knows without revealing the secret of Jack Shadow's identity.

"I haven't much to steal Mr Finch," Ruby says.

"No doubt he would leave you alone anyhow, as you've a highwayman in the family."

Ruby is suddenly wide awake. Has Finch guessed? "What do you mean?"

"I meant no offence," says Sam Finch, seeing that he has hit a raw nerve. "There's plenty would be proud to have old Ned Sharpe as an ancestor."

Ruby smiles with relief. She never knew her uncle, Ned Sharpe. He met his end long before she had been born and Lizzie Gilbert was always tight lipped about her infamous brother. Everyone knows the stories:

Ned Sharpe was an honest farmer until he fell foul of the law. In a tavern brawl over a game of cards a man was killed. No one knows who struck the fateful blow but it was Ned who was blamed. It didn't matter that Ned had fought in self defence, nor did it matter that the dead man had begun the fight by firing his pistol at Ned when Ned had caught him slipping an extra ace from his sleeve. The dead man had been the son of a Lord and someone had to hang for his murder. With no hope of justice, Ned ran to the hills and chose the life of an outlaw.

As a highwayman, Ned Sharpe became the terror of the coach roads from Bristol to Penzance. By the time he was caught, Ned Sharpe had killed more than a dozen men. For all that, he was well loved, for he was always free-handed with his loot and kept many poor families from starvation with his charity. The songs and tales all painted him as a tragic hero. Would anyone make up songs about Jack Shadow? Ruby hoped not; songs like that never had a happy ending.

Ruby did not want to die at the end of a rope like Ned Sharpe. She was resolved; it was time to put an end to Jack Shadow. She had enough gold hidden away to look after her family. Ruby would miss the thrill of it but there was no sense in taking any more risks. The stakes were too high.

Ruby is startled from her thoughts by the sudden shying of the horses. A hare bobs through the hedge in front of the cart and races along the road ahead of them.

"That's one of Mab's brood, I'll be bound," says Farmer Finch. "Off to whisper all our secrets to the Queen of Shadows."

"Do you believe in those old tales?" asked Ruby.

"Some of those stories might be more fanciful than sensible, but I wouldn't like to say I don't believe in them," says Finch."I saw something once, when I was a lad, that I have never forgotten nor made sense of:

"I was walking in Fiddler's wood one morning, just about this time of day, when I heard the most beautiful music coming up from the Folly Brook. I turned to follow the sound and I spied a fellow, all dressed in green clothes, sitting on a rock by the stream. He was tiny as a child but with the face of a full grown man with long grey hair. He had a broken harp over his shoulder and was playing the lovely music on a tiny flute. I never heard such a song; it made me want to laugh, cry and dance, all at the same time.

I stood there, listening to the music and staring at the little fellow with my eyes fair popping out of my head and then I thought I might get closer. I'd a notion that he was most likely a Faerie and there might be something to be gained if I could get hold of him. As I stepped forward the sun caught me in the eyes and I was dazzled. When I was done blinking the fellow was gone and where he had been there was only a sparrow. The strangest thing was; I could have sworn that the sparrow was holding a bit of bulrush in its claws, carved like a tiny flute."

"Do you think the Faerie turned into a bird?" asks Ruby.

"The old tales often tell how the Fair folk can change shape," replies Finch with a twinkle in his eye. "They come as birds or animals, just as they please, but my grandma told me that they most often like to come in the shape of a hare - which is why it's bad luck to shoot one."

"I'll tell my brother to be more careful when he's out hunting," says Ruby.

Farmer Finch's story makes Ruby smile. She knew plenty of others like it and has never taken them for anything other than tall tales. In the warm sunlight, the things she saw last night seem a long way off. Surely the things written in the Keys of Queen Mab are just superstition, like the tales that Finch's grandma had told him. The Squire believes in them, perhaps, and they had lead him to do terrible things, but he would not be the first man to fall in thrall to the empty promise of magic.

By the time they reach Truro the market square is busy; the usual market crowds swelled by travellers who have come for the great gathering at Summercourt Fair, only a week away. Ruby and Davey help Farmer Finch set up his stall and head off into the crowd.

Ruby's first errand is to the pawnbroker. She pauses and pulls Davey aside under the shade of the Market Oak. She takes the Keys of Queen Mab from her bundle.

"How much do you think I should ask for this?" she asks, putting the book into Davey's hand.

He turns it over, admiring the gold leaf patterns on the cover. There are three keys, each one with the head of an animal: a horse, a hawk and a hare. Davey opens the book to the title page.

"The Keys of Queen Mab." He looks up at Ruby inquiringly. "Was this your mother's?"

"No," says Ruby. She has resolved to tell Davey the truth from now on, as far as she can. Now is not the time to tell it all, perhaps later on, once they were home from the market. "I can't tell you how I came by it, " she says."Is it valuable?"

"It looks old," says Davey. "A pawnbroker wouldn't give you much for it but if you take it to a bookseller in Plymouth you'd get a fair price."

Ruby looks down at the book; the Squire clearly wanted it badly, Mr Periwigge had said as much, and now that she has seen the scorched fragments at Colby Hall she had an idea why. Perhaps it would be better to burn it?

It seems wrong to destroy something so beautiful. She will keep it for the moment and take it to Plymouth some day when she needs the money.

"Look after it for me," says Ruby, "but promise that you'll keep it secret."

"Of course"

Davey didn't understand - how could he? Just holding the book put him in danger. But if he read some of it then perhaps it would be easier to explain about the Squire?

"Don't show it to a living soul!" Ruby says fiercely.

"I promise."

When Ruby is gone, Davey finds a secluded place under the Market Oak to sit and read.

The book's author does not give his name but he claims to have travelled to Faerie and seen all it's wonders and perils first hand.

"The Lands of Faery reach through all of time, to the very edge of dreaming and the gates of death. The dead may be found there, and the Gods. The rulers of Faerie call themselves the Sidhe. They are immortals and to them our brief lives seem to pass in the blink of an eye. One, alone among the Sidhe, pays any mind to the mortal realm; Queen Mab, the perilous and beautiful ruler of them all.

Queen Mab sends her servants to the Waking World in the form of animals. They pass among us unknown and on their return they come to sit at the Queen's feet and tell her all that they have seen. Many tales she hears and much she learns, and sometimes, very seldom, she is moved to interfere in the affairs of mortals. The Faerie Queen has a great fondness for poets and musicians and there is little help for any mortal youth who she sets her charm upon; they are called to Faerie to be her minstrels and seen no more in the Waking World."

The following pages are filled with charms and spells; spells for the summoning of a Faery servant, for spinning clothes from the wind, charms of forgetting and charms of finding, riddles to confound tigers, and notes on the languages of moles and owls. There are other, more sinister things; the method of binding a human heart, the fashioning of a bridle for a nightmare and the commanding of speech from bones. The spells are made up of short poems in a language that Davey has never seen before. There is a curious music to the rhymes and he takes out his notebook to copy some of them down.

Davey is startled by a sudden chill. The sun has slipped behind a cloud and he is suddenly aware of an eerie humming sound nearby. He looks up to see a tall man standing before him. The man is as thin as a rake, his dark clothes hanging off his bones like torn flags. He meets Davey's enquiring look with his sparkling blue eyes and holds his gaze. Slung over the man's shoulder is a weatherbeaten wooden box. There is slot in the front of the box and a tarnished silver handle on the side, which the old man is winding slowly in his large, bony hand. He turns the handle harder and the plaintive wailing of the hurdy gurdy rises.

The old man's voice is high and sweet and the words of his song blend seamlessly with the music of the hurdy gurdy. The man sings in a strange, lilting language and the music that he makes tells of joy, grief and wonder.

The scarecrow man looks down at the book and winks at Davey, then turns away, winding his way through the crowd. Not many seem to notice him but Davey sees one old woman bow her head to the singer and place a silver coin into the slot on the front of the box. Davey watches him out of sight, spellbound by the music.

"You'll catch a fly if you sit like that," says Ruby, flopping down beside him on the bench. Davey blinks and closes his mouth. It seems as if Ruby has only been away a moment but she must have been gone a good while. She has already been to the pawnshop and has a parcel in her hands with new shoes in it for Katy.

The pawnbroker had asked far too many questions for Ruby's liking and she'd taken a poor price for the snuffbox. She was glad that she hadn't brought any of the other things. With the price on Jack Shadow's head it was dangerous to sell any of his loot.

"Who was that ragamuffin?" Ruby asks, looking after the hurdy gurdy man.

"I'm not sure . . ." begins Davey, still half entranced by the strange music.

"Stop dozing and come and help," Ruby says. " I can't carry all this on my own. I need some bags of seed and I've got to get a couple of new hens before we go home."

Davey slips the book into his coat pocket and lets Ruby drag him away into the bustle of the market place. He looks for the hurdy gurdy player in the crowd but he is gone. There are plenty of other distractions; sugar apples to be eaten and hens to be bought. When Ruby has done all her errands they stop to eat pasties and watch a puppet show in a booth beside a brightly painted caravan. The marionette play is of St.George and the Dragon, though it seems to be a different tale to the one Davey knows. St.George wears a crown of leaves and has horns like a goat and he does not slay the dragon but subdues it with a charm that he has learned from the silver eyed Lady of the Moon.

As the crowd begins to thin out, Davey remembers his own errand and runs to buy writing paper and ink from the shop behind the market square. By then, the day is almost gone and they are soon jogging home again in Finch's wagon, going faster now, with all his baskets empty.

   They have all been up since before dawn and Farmer Finch begins to nod off as he drives. Ruby falls asleep on Davey's shoulder but Davey remains wide awake. He cannot shake off the uneasy feeling that came over him in the market place and the plaintive song of the hurdy gurdy man seems to follow them as they go. As they crest a rise in the road, Davey looks back to see if the beggar is following them but the road is empty. He asks Farmer Finch if he hears the music, but he shakes his head.

Chapter 16.

They jump off the cart at the bottom of Gilbert's Lane and walk up the hill together. Davey is in no hurry to return to the vicarage and Ruby has invited him up to the cottage for supper.

They are half way up the hill when they catch the smell of burning. They look up to see smoke rising from the top of the hill like pale summer mist.

"No!" says Ruby, her heart lurching with panic. "It can't be . . "

She takes off up the hill with Davey close behind her.

Ruby turns the corner and halts. Gilbert's Cottage is a smoking ruin. The stone walls are still standing but the roof and everything else that can burn has been charred to cinders. Ruby can feel the fierce heat of the smouldering house on her face but, inside, it as if she had been plunged into deep water, bottomless and freezing. Her eyes sting with smoke and tears but she is so numb that she hardly feels it. Everything that has ever mattered to her took place in Gilbert's Cottage - her whole life. Now it is gone.

There is a cry behind her and Ruby turns to see Katy running from the wood, her soot stained face streaked with tears. Behind her comes Mrs. Finch, pale and sorrowful. Katy runs to Ruby's side and buries her face in her dress.

"What happened?" asks Ruby, in a dazed voice, her hand absently stroking Katy's hair.

"They came and took Dad and Tom away," says Katy."Then they burned down the house. The Squire said that Tom's that highwayman, Jack Shadow!"

"They can't have!" Exclaims Ruby, her eyes wild with confusion.

"Thank the Lord you're back, Ruby," says Mrs. Finch. "The men came up from the Tithe Cottages and put out the fire. They managed to save the barn but it was too late for the cottage. We've taken Jet and Bessie down to the farm. You're welcome there too, Ruby, for as long as you need to stay."

"What about my father and Tom?"

"The soldiers came for Tom. They took Seth too, when he tried to shoot them."

"How could they do that?"

"They found the things in the barn, a ring and a silver pistol."

Ruby is already running through the smoke.

Davey follows, and catches up with her at the back of the barn. The apple boxes have been thrown aside and the floorboards ripped up. There is a hole in the earth at Ruby's feet, lined with sacking.

"How could I have been so stupid," she says staring down into the empty hole, "I should have moved those things." She glances up to hayloft, squinting into the darkness. She takes a step towards the hayloft ladder and looks up into the shadows. She is about to climb the ladder but notices Davey standing in the door and stops in her tracks.

"What is it?" Davey asks.

Ruby shakes her head, puts her face in her hands and begins to sob. Davey comes to her side and puts a tentative hand onto her shoulder.

"It's a mistake," he says." Tom's no highwayman."

Ruby just sobs harder.

She promised her mother that she would look after her family but in her foolishness and arrogance she has put them in the worst kind of danger. What can she do now? She has failed them all.

Ruby steps back from Davey, brushing the tears from her face.

"Don't think badly of me," she says. "You mean the world to me and I couldn't bear for you to hate me."

"What do you mean? I never could think anything bad of you -"

"You don't know anything!"

"Tell me."

"It's a terrible thing to be poor, Davey, not to know where your next meal is coming from. There are things that you have to do. You could never understand."

Davey is stung by her words. He blushes and looked down at his boots.

Ruby sees Davey's expression and turns away from him, furious with herself. She isn't angry with Davey - he's the last person to blame. She is so stupid - all she ever does is hurt the people she cares most about!

There is only one way to put things right; Ruby's blood runs cold at the thought of it but there is nothing else to be done. She takes a deep breath and turns back to face Davey.

"I'll just have to go and tell them who Jack Shadow really is. They'll hang Tom and Seth if I don't"

"I'll come with you."

"No!" Ruby fixes Davey with a fierce look. "You stay here look after Katy until my father comes back." She steps forward, kisses him on the cheek and runs from the barn.

Davey stands looking after Ruby as she disappears down the lane. Katy tries to run after her but Mrs Finch grabs her up and holds her back. Davey wants to follow Ruby too but she was so adamant that he should remain behind. He tries to make sense of what had happened. Ruby clearly knows who Jack Shadow is. Does that mean that she is in league with him? Davey remembers the glance Ruby took up into the the hayloft and the way she stepped away from the ladder when she saw him.

It doesn't take long for Davey to climb up and find the loose stone in the wall. In gap behind the stone is a bundle of clothes. It weighs heavy in his hands as he pulls it out and as Davey unrolls the cloak several objects fall out onto the straw: a black hat, a scarf, a powder horn and a leather shoulder belt with three holstered pistols. When Davey lifts the hat, a blue ribbon falls out onto the straw. The ribbon is Ruby's.

Jack Shadow must be Ruby's sweetheart! Davey feels a surge of jealous rage and throws the hat away across the loft. It sails through the air and bounces back off the wall to fall at his feet. He stands for a moment, scowling, then gathers up the things and puts them back in their hiding place. Whatever the truth, he cannot let Ruby turn herself in. If she has been harbouring a highwayman then she will face the hangman; there has to be another way.

Ruby has a good start on Davey and he doesn't catch up with her until she is already at the courthouse. A crowd has gathered in the village square where a group of soldiers stand guard at the door of the jail. Ruby is at the front of the crowd.
"You can't take Tom," she shouts. "He's only a boy!"
The sergeant in charge is stoney-faced.
"He's man enough to hang. Perhaps your father will get lucky and the Magistrate will let him live. Transportation is a damn sight better than the rope."
"I'll tell you who Jack Shadow is," says Ruby.
The sergeant laughs. "Give it up miss. It was the Squire himself found the booty in the barn. I saw him do it with my own eyes."
"You don't understand. Just let me speak to the Squire."
"You'll see him at the trial, " the sergeant says gruffly.
Ruby tries to push past the soldiers but Davey has his hand on her shoulder by then and he pulls her back.
"You'll do no good with this."
She shrugs Davey off and pushes forward again. There are angry murmurs from the crowd and several men step forward to Ruby's side. John Summer, the blacksmith, is there with a heavy forge hammer in his hand and a hot rage in his eyes:
"Seth Gilbert's no robber, " he growls. "There's no more honest man in England. We don't like to see innocent men taken, whatever the Magistrate might have to say about it."
The soldiers take a step back at the sight of the hammer and the menace in the blacksmith's voice.

They lower their rifles, pointing them at the oncoming men.

"They will have a fair trial," barks the Sergeant. "Meanwhile, the first man to take another step will be shot. Interfering with the servants of the King is treason." He raises his hand and glances back at his men.

Davey drags Ruby back into the crowd:

"I know your secret," he hisses into her ear. "We'll find a way to help them, but you have to come with me - now!"

Ruby turns to look at Davey, the strength suddenly seeming to go out of her.

"Come on," Davey says, taking Ruby by the arm and leading her away to the far side of the square. There are more raised voices behind them but the crowd stays back and the soldiers hold their fire.

The passage along the side of the church is deserted and Davey leads Ruby down to the edge of the churchyard.

"I know that Jack Shadow is your sweetheart," Davey says, blushing as he forces himself to meet Ruby's gaze." I found the other things in the barn, the cloak and the pistols. But there is no use turning him in. He would most likely just run and then there would be no proof to clear Tom's name." Davey pauses. He cannot read Ruby's expression, she just stands staring at him, open mouthed. "The best way to save Tom is for Jack Shadow to be seen again, while he and your father are locked up in the jail. The Magistrate won't be able to hold them then. Jack

Shadow will just have to rob someone tonight. Can you contact him?"

Ruby stares at Davey, dumbfounded.

At last, she nods, understanding slowly dawning on her face:

"You're right. Jack Shadow can help us." Then she throws her arms about Davey's neck and kisses him. She pulls back, smiling. "You're wrong about one thing; Jack Shadow isn't my sweetheart."

"He's not?"

"No, you lumphead! It's me, I'm Jack Shadow!"

Chapter 17.

The only topic of conversation at the White Horse that night is that of the Highwayman.
"Tom was always a wild one, like all of them Gilberts," says Ben Rushton." It doesn't surprise me he's come to a bad end. Everyone knows what happened to his uncle."
"I've heard the lad was in with the smugglers," puts in another man.
"Tom Gilbert's no robber," replies John Summer. He glares at the stranger, who hurriedly turns away. "And you're a fool, Ben Rushton, if you believe it." Ben Rushton shrugs but chooses not to argue with the Blacksmith.
"It's that poor lass Ruby I feel sorry for," says Mrs Carrick, bustling up to the table to smooth things over. "She's lost her mother and now her father and brother too. It's more than any soul should have to bear. To think of her alone now, with nowhere to call her home and her little sister no more than a baby - it breaks my heart." She dabs a tear away from her eye.

If Mrs Carrick knew what Ruby was up to at that very moment then she might have felt rather differently.

Ruby ties the sacking around Caliban's feet, before moving on to the other horses. They will need three of them in all, one each for her and Davey and another for Seth and Tom. She has chosen Dervish, the Squire's chestnut mare, for Davey. He should be able to handle her. Tom is not a natural horseman and for him she needs a beast that will follow the others, rather than get any ideas of its own. She has settled on Molly, a solid looking grey carriage horse. Stealing from the Manor is a risk but it is the only way - the only other horses to be had in the valley belong to honest men. The thought of how vexed Squire Colby will be to find them gone is just a bonus.

* * * *

It takes Davey some while to get over the shock of Ruby's revelation.
"Why Ruby?" he asks, at last.
"I'll tell you. But not here."
She leads him through the graveyard, to the place behind the Yew tree and they sit, side by side against the wall.
"I know I've been a fool," Ruby begins. "But hear me out before you condemn me."
Davey nods.
Ruby takes a deep breath and begins;
"It was so hard after my mother died. She left us so suddenly and my father was still weak from his accident. We all thought he would give in and die of grief after she was buried.

It was a cruel winter and there was no money for food. Tom went hunting sometimes but the rest was up to me. Everyone around us was kind: John Summer, Mrs Carrick and Farmer Finch - they gave all that they could spare but I couldn't carry on asking for charity from our neighbours.

The Squire was busy ruining the valley and there was precious little work be had in the village, so I took Katy to the Finch's, left Tom to care for my father and went to Plymouth. But there was no work to be found in Plymouth either. The towns are all full of poor girls from the country, trying to make their way. Some lucky ones find places as maids, while the rest fall to being beggars, or worse. When my money ran out I was forced to start begging myself, just to get a bite to eat. I lived for two weeks like that - two weeks of being spat on by passersby and threatened by the other poor wretches who shared my position.

I was just set to give it all up and come home when something happened that changed everything.

I was sitting in a doorway, sheltering from the rain, when I saw a carriage pull up across the street. A well dressed Lady and Gentleman came out of a grand house and I started toward the carriage, hoping they might give me a Farthing.

Another beggar had been watching from nearby and she beat me to it. I recognised the beggar woman, her name was Florrie. She was one of the few people who had shown me any kindness, sharing a crust of bread with me one day when I was truly desperate. Her situation was even worse than mine; her husband had died and, though she was only a few years older than me, she had two tiny children to care for.

Florrie ran forward and threw herself at the Gentleman's feet, pulling at his coat, but the rich fellow simply threw her aside and let her fall into the gutter. As he ordered the coachman to set off, I saw that Florrie would be crushed under the carriage wheels. I ran forward and got there just in time to pull her clear.

As I helped Florrie to her feet, I looked up and caught the eye of the man in the carriage. He only held my gaze for an instant but in that moment I saw all that I needed to see. The self-satisfied expression on his face, the complete lack of pity in his eyes. The smallest ring on his finger would have fed Florrie's whole family for a year and yet he sat there in his fine carriage with his prim lady wife and her perfumed lapdog, not giving a thought for poor Florrie, not caring a jot if she lived or died.

I'm not one for sermons, Davey, but there is one passage that I remember from the Bible; it says that a rich man is as likely to enter the kingdom of heaven as a camel is to pass through a needle's eye. I never understood it before but now I'd say that there's never been a truer word spoken. I saw how little goodness there is in the hearts of men and how little justice there is in the world for those not lucky enough to be born rich. My mother brought me up to believe in providence - to believe that good things come to those who do good. Her life and death gave the lie to that . . ." Ruby wipes away a tear and Davey waits for her to continue.

"As I rode away from Plymouth on the back of a cart the next day I was sick at heart and burning with fury. It was then that it came to me - how I might make my own providence. I was light-headed with hunger and the thought of it made me laugh out loud. The carter must have thought me half mad. Perhaps it was madness - it seems like it now; To be a highwayman! To do my bit to even up the crookedness of the world. I'd heard stories of Ned Sharpe and them other cutting rogues all my life and I'd thought them nothing but high tales. But I understood then how someone might be driven to it.

Only a few days before, a fellow had robbed two rich gentlemen right before my eyes. The robber just stepped up to the men, bold as brass, put his pistol in their faces and called for their valuables. The two gentlemen gave him all they had and ran for it, even though the thief was alone and a scrawny little fellow at that.

As the robber made off along the alley he tripped up on the cobbles and fell at my feet. The scarf fell from his face and I saw that he was a boy, no more than ten years old and scared out of his wits. I knew that if a trembling lad could pull off such a robbery, then I could make a good fist of it.

As soon as I got home I went to my grandfather's old sea chest and took out his travelling cloak and black hat. As I rummaged at the bottom for something to make myself a mask I found a bundle wrapped in white lace. The lace was my mother's wedding dress and rolled up in it were three pistols. Her family had been farmers, all save one, and I fancy the pistols must have belonged to him.

Ned Sharpe's, or not, I took the finding of the guns as a sign that I was doing the right thing.

I racked my brains to find a horse. I couldn't use old Bess, or any other one that would be recognised. Then I remembered Caliban. The Squire has never managed to stay on his back. That's because he tried to gain mastery of him - to break his spirit. That is not my way. Caliban lets me ride him because he knows that I can give him his freedom. He listens to me because I do not seek to own or control him."

Davey smiles. He has no doubt that it is true. He remembers how Ruby learned to ride before she could walk, her father sitting her on the back of a horse as he walked along beside her. Davey remembers too, the times that Ruby took him up onto the moors to see the wild ponies. He never dared to ride one but he had watched her fearlessly befriend them, wrapping her hands into their matted manes and laughing with delight as they carried her leaping over the heather.

"Taking the Squire's prize stallion from under his nose has a sweetness to it and he carries me as swift as the wind itself. What better mount for a highwayman?" Ruby smiles, a glitter of wildness coming into her eyes. "That first time I held up a coach I was so terrified that I sat shaking in the saddle, barely able to hold the pistols steady. I could barely speak for my chattering teeth. No one saw that though, they only saw the wild snorting horse, the gun and the mask. As I watched the bacon-fed, terrified faces of those London gentlemen handing over their gold I felt a thrill of something rare and true; I was no longer just a poor farmer's daughter who had to scrimp and struggle for every farthing. I had a hand on the scales of justice and I could tip them, just a little, in the right direction.

It's a strange thing, but once people saw my mask I fancy that they imagined all their worst fears hid behind it. It worked like a charm and I never had any trouble with those I robbed. I certainly never came near shooting anyone. I'm glad of that, for I had promised myself that I shouldn't cause hurt and I kept my pistols loaded only to frighten.

   Those times when I rode the moor dressed as Jack Shadow, I felt as if I were another person. I was free and strong and I answered to no-one. As the months passed and I wasn't caught I began to believe that I was charmed. I think that I took a notion that I was like one of those knights in those stories that my mother used to tell me, chivalrous heroes who were pure of heart and could defeat terrible enemies."
Ruby shakes her head. "Foolish, all of it."
"There's not many who would have the courage to do what you've done" Davey says."To most people round here you're a hero."
"And to you?"
"I'd say you're a hero."
Ruby looks away, not wanting him to see the relief on her face.
"I'm lucky I didn't get shot myself," she says." But now Tom and my father are in the jail because of me. There's no good in that."
Davey shrugs. "We'll just have to rescue them."
"I'm in this up to my neck,"says Ruby."But there's no reason for you to get involved."
"I'm already involved."
"You'd risk becoming an outlaw, with a price on your head."
"I've no intention of becoming a vicar, or a Notary clerk, or whatever else my father has in mind. "

"I've brought all this down on my family. It's up to me to sort it out," says Ruby.

"You can't do it alone, can you?"

Davey is right - Ruby knows it. Rescuing Tom and Seth will take more than one person, even if that person is Jack Shadow. Besides, she wants Davey with her. It was only as she shared her secrets with Davey that Ruby realised how hard they had been to bear alone.

By the evening they have hatched a plan. It won't be enough for Jack Shadow to simply appear again; the silver pistol and the other things that the Squire found in the barn were fairly damning; Seth and Tom could easily be hanged for that. Even if it was shown that they had arrested the wrong men, Ruby knows that Josia Colby would not relinquish them. He wants Seth Gilbert's land too much.

The only solution is for Jack Shadow to rescue Tom and Seth himself. If all goes to plan then they will be fugitives, but it is a far better prospect than suffering the Squire's twisted justice. The world is wide and there are other places than Bascome to live.

*   *   *   *

Davey waits now at the end of the stable, ready to warn Ruby if the stableman wakes up. There seems little danger of it. The old man is snoring mightily as he slumps in his seat by the door, an empty cider jug at his side. The handful of Valerian root that Ruby slipped into the drink has done it's work.

When Ruby has muffled the horses hooves with sacking she leads them, one by one, out of the back doors of the stable and ties them to the fence. She begins with the quiet carriage horse and leaves Caliban till last, as he is the most likely to raise a fuss. Once all three horses are out, Davey joins her and they set them off into the forest.

The woods are silent but as Ruby and Davey pause in a clearing to mount up there is a flutter of wings. As the bird flies across the face of the moon Davey sees the silhouette of a hawk. It is strange to see one flying at night? He has no time to ponder on it. Ruby is waiting up ahead, wearing the mask of Jack Shadow.

Chapter 18.

Private Alfie Clough is on guard at the door of the jail. The night is quiet and he can hear the sound of merry voices coming up from the inn at the bottom of the hill. His thoughts turn wistfully to the subject of Mrs. Carrick's cider. On any other night he might chance nipping down for a swift mug but he doesn't dare risk it. The sergeant will have Alfie's guts for garters if he is discovered away from his post while the infamous Jack Shadow is in the cells. Truth be told, Alfie can't see that scared looking boy as a highwayman, but no one is asking for his opinion. They just ask him to stand by the door all night without a bite to eat and keep a lookout. He does his best to ignore the rumbling in his belly and stamps his feet to bring the circulation back into his legs.

Alfie hears the scuffle of boots on the stone flagging behind him but he turns too late; a hand is clamped over his mouth and a cold blade pressed to his throat. "Hold your tongue - if you want to live!" hisses a voice in his ear.
The black cloaked figure makes short work of tying the soldier's arms and gagging him with a cloth, before dragging him off into the shadows.

Sergeant Wilks is roused from his slumber by a thunderous hammering on the door of the Jail. Cursing mightily, he pulls on his boots and takes up his pistol. In the guardroom he kicks the troopers out of their beds, before stomping to the door.

"Is that you Clough?" he calls out, as he buttons up his braces. "What is it man?"

"Open up sir," comes a voice, muffled through the thick door." I've an urgent message from Squire Colby. He says it won't wait."

Sergeant Wilks takes the keys from his belt and unlocks the jailhouse door.

Instead of Alfie Clough in the doorway, there is a black clad figure with a scarf over his face. The highwayman levels two pistol barrels at Sergeant Wilks' chest. The Sergeant's own pistol is in his hand but he has not had the time to load it. His sword is still hanging by his bed.

"Jack Shadow, at your service." The highwayman bows and inclines his head. "I have come to set the record straight and let you know that you've got the wrong men locked up in your jail."

Behind him Sergeant Wilks can hear the other troopers clattering about in the guardroom, bumping into each other in their hurry to pull on their boots and gather up their rifles. He opens his mouth to call out to them but the masked man gestures meaningfully with a jab of his pistols and Wilks thinks better of it.

"I couldn't let an innocent fellow go dance a jig with Captain Swing on my account," says the masked man. "Perhaps you'd be good enough to set them free, Sergeant, then you can get back to your beauty sleep."

"Your accomplices will hang with you," growls Sergeant Wilks." We'll just have to build more gibbets on Reavers Hill."

"I was afraid that you'd say that," says Jack Shadow, raising his guns.

The pistol shot is deafeningly loud in the enclosed space of the jailhouse doorway and the Sergeant is half blinded by the flash of the powder. He falls back, tripping over his braces and hitting his head on the flagstones. He lies there for a long moment, dazed and waiting to die.

"Sergeant, are you hit?" comes a tentative voice.

Apart from a sharp throbbing in the back of his head, Wilks isn't in any great pain. The Sergeant reaches up and feels his chest and then, rather sheepishly, gets to his feet. The pistol shot missed him, or the ruffian had aimed high on purpose.

"Step to it!" Sergeant Wilks yells at his bleary eyed troopers. "Get your rifles and follow me!"

In the town square there seems to be no sign of the highwayman. Then there comes a loud whinny from behind the church and a black stallion gallops into view. The rider slows as he passes and lifts his hat.

"Catch me if you can. Are you men enough for the chase?" the rider laughs, before kicking the horse forward and galloping away down the hill so fast that the iron shoes strike sparks from the cobbles.

Sergeant Wilks curses; their own horses are stabled down at the inn and the scoundrel will be half way to Truro by the time they get after him. The Sergeant throws aside his useless pistol and grabs a rifle from one of his troopers. Hefting it to his shoulder he lets fly but he is too vexed to aim properly and the shot goes wide. The other soldiers raise their guns and fire but the rider is out of range by then, clattering away down the cobbled street.

"Get to the horses and ride after him!" shouts the Sergeant.

   Davey has been waiting in the shadows, watching for Ruby's signal. When he sees her lift her hat, he steps back into the yard at the back of the Courthouse and jumps onto the back of the Squire's chestnut mare. The grey coach horse is beside them and a rope runs back from each of the saddles to the bars of the jail cell. Davey urges the horses forward as hard as he can and the rope springs tight. Both horses snort at the sudden pull and for a moment it looks as if the rope might snap under the strain. There is a shriek of iron grating on stone, a loud crack and the bars of the cells are wrenched free of the wall. Dust and stone chippings fly as the bars, along with a chunk of the walls, fall to the ground with a crash.

   Davey has already whispered news of the plan through the bars to Seth and Tom and they are out in an instant and up onto the grey horse's back.

   The soldiers are halfway to the inn when they hear the clamour of the falling wall. Sergeant Wilks roars with fury as he realises how he has been tricked and he turns to lead his men haring back up the hill.

   By the time they get back to the jail the prisoners are long gone.

Chapter 19.

Davey, Tom and Seth meet up with Ruby at the edge of Fiddler's Wood. Ruby dismounts and goes to Seth where he sits behind Tom on the grey coach horse.
"Are you alright father?"
"Better for hearing your voice, lass."
Ruby helps Seth down from the horse and hugs him hard.
"I'm sorry for everything I've done. I promised mother that I'd look after you and all I've done is make everything worse. I've been a fool."
Seth frowns and shakes his head. "Your mother would be proud of you."
Tom nods in agreement.
"But the cottage . . . " begins Ruby.
"The Squire has been set upon turfing us out of Gilbert's Cottage ever since I can remember," says Seth. "And he would have found a way to do it, sooner or later, whatever we did." He takes Ruby's hand and speaks softly. "The cottage was only old stones. We can make a new home, somewhere else."
Ruby has not considered what they might do next. She has thought only of rescuing Seth and Tom.
"If we run away then the Squire will have driven us out," she says. "We can't let him do that."
"We're all for the rope if they catch us now. But if we escape then we live to fight another day. Perhaps, one day, we'll come back, but there's no place for us here, unless we live out on the moors like bandits."
Ruby nods. If she were alone, then Ruby might do just that, but the moors are a cruel place to live in

winter and Seth and Katy would not last long.
Besides, what kind of life would it be - always on the run, never able to trust anyone.

"Ketch Avery says there's more than one ship's captain owes him a favour," says Tom. "We might get a passage to France."

"I didn't know you was so thick with Ketch Avery," says Seth sharply, turning to scowl at his son.

Tom makes no reply. He sees how old and careworn his father is.

"It's just as well that Tom is in with the smugglers," says Ruby." If it means they can get us safely out of here."

"There's a cave, near the Pikestone," says Tom." Ketch uses it for a hideaway. We can lie low there until we know our next move."

"Good lad. What about Katy?"

"She's safe," says Davey. "Mrs. Finch will look after her until we come for her."

Ruby puts a hand on her father's arm. "You ride with Davey and give Tom's horse a rest."

Ruby would have preferred to take Seth herself but she isn't sure that her father will want to ride Caliban, or whether the stallion will submit to it. The black horse stands calmly and, as Seth comes close, he tosses his head and gives a snort of greeting. Seth turns toward the sound. Putting aside Ruby's arm, he steps to Caliban's side, running his hand gently down the horse's neck. He murmurs something under his breath and Caliban stands patiently, allowing himself to be stroked, lowering his head and making soft snorting noises. Ruby watches her father lean toward the black stallion's head. She cannot guess what he is feeling. It is the first time that he has been close to Caliban since that fateful day in the stable.

As Seth stands beside Caliban, a calmness falls about them all. Davey and Tom watch in silence and the other horses fall quiet as something passes between the blind man and the dark horse, a mystery too deep and wild to be shaped into words.

"The Troopers will be on our trail before long," Seth says. "We should go."

Ruby leads her father to the chestnut mare, who greets Seth with a friendly snicker. Davey helps Seth up behind him and they ride on.

On the far side of the wood they ford the river and take a path up a rocky valley toward the foot of the moor, keeping close to the thickets of gorse and hawthorn that cluster along the stream bank.

Suddenly Tom calls them to a halt, pointing up to the ragged line of the moor edge, half a mile ahead of them. Silhouettes move against the stars; a line of soldiers, the long barrels of their rifles clearly visible. Even as they halt, there is a flash of powder and a gunshot echoes across the valley. A moment later comes the sound of galloping horses from behind them and a group of mounted soldiers break free from the trees.

"We've ridden into a trap!" says Ruby." We're done for if we don't act fast." She glances up at the men on the hilltop. There are not many of them - six at most - but there are twenty riders; too many to fight. The

mounted soldiers are still a quarter of a mile away and there is a chance that they can outrun them.
"Davey, you and Tom take Seth and go on foot," Ruby says. "You'll be hidden by the trees and you can get over to the Pikestone at the top. Tom knows the path. I'll take the horses and ride out over the moor in the opposite direction. They'll see the horses and follow me. I can easily outride them on Caliban and meet you all at the hideout."
Tom nods and slips down from the saddle of the grey horse.
"I'm coming with you," says Davey. "The troopers might not notice one riderless horse but two will make them suspicious."
"I'll go faster alone".
"Do as he says, lass," says Seth. "Dervish will keep pace with Caliban. She's a fiery girl, like you. And I'd feel better if Davey was there to look after you."
"You seem to have forgotten that I am the infamous brigand, Jack Shadow!" Ruby laughed. "I don't need protecting."
"Brigand or not," says Seth. "Davey's right. Two riderless horses will look wrong."
There is no time to argue. Ruby takes the reins of the grey horse and Tom leads Seth into the cover of the gorse bushes. Once they are safely out of sight, Ruby turns Caliban about and kicks him forward.
"Keep close Davey!"

The mounted soldiers are on the flat of the valley bottom and gaining fast, while Ruby and Davey have to scale the steep hillside to the moor top. They have to hope that the pursuers' horses are no match for Caliban and Dervish.

As they climb the valley side, Ruby hears the thud of the soldiers' horses on the slope behind. Up ahead, the troopers at the moor edge began to move toward them, drawing the pursuit away from Tom and Seth. Caliban pulls hard at his bridle, eager to leave the soldiers far behind, but Ruby holds him back. She wants to keep the soldiers near and lead them as far away from Seth and Tom as she can. They scramble to the moor edge, find a path and gallop. Minutes later the troopers are after them, riding hard over the heather. Ruby gives Caliban a freer rein then and he plunges forward, hooves thudding like thunder on the path. Davey does the same and Dervish follows, matching the stallion's pace.

After a couple of miles the path turns down toward Claypit Woods. Ruby slows Caliban to a trot and turns to look back over her shoulder. The troopers are still behind them, two hundred yards away. Ruby flashes Davey a wild grin. Davey knows that look well; it means that trouble is on the way.
"It's time to leave them behind," Ruby says, kicking Caliban forward. "Hold on tight!" As Caliban leaps away down the track, Ruby leans forward in the saddle and presses her face against his neck. "Run for all you are worth! "
The stallion races into a headlong gallop, so swift and fierce that it is almost as if he has taken flight. The wind rushes in Ruby's ears and the trees are lost in a haze of speed. The pale ribbon of the path fades as

they fly over it and she sees only the starlight glinting in Caliban's night dark eye.

Dervish is left to run in Caliban's dust, doing her best to match his furious pace. Davey leans forward, as he saw Ruby do. He wraps his fingers into the chestnut mane and does his best not to scream; galloping downhill in the dark at breakneck speed with branches whizzing by only inches away is utterly terrifying and he soon gives up any pretence of guiding his horse, concentrating instead on trying to stay in the saddle.

At the bottom of the hill, Ruby reins Caliban in, they slow and she turns him down a side track. Davey and Dervish follow behind and they halt behind a thicket of holly, lie against their horses necks and wait.

The soldiers ride straight by, too intent upon the chase to notice them in the shadows. They pass close enough for Ruby and Davey to see the moonlight glittering on the buttons of their red coats as they gallop down toward the main highway.

Ruby and Davey lead their horses on foot. They keep their eyes and ears sharp and for a long while they hear nothing but the whisper of wind and the soft night noises of the wood. The summer trees give good cover and the shadows lie in deep blue-black pools, lit here and there with bright drifts of moonlight. Once they are halted by a harsh cry nearby and look up to see a swift, winged shape lift away from the trees ahead. Silence falls once more and they carry on more quickly, in case the sound of the startled bird has alerted the troopers.

Ruby leads them up into a gully where a stream falls into a wide pool. There they halt to rest and let their horses drink.

Chapter 20.

Ruby splashes water on her face and stands up. The moon is setting, which means that there are only a couple of hours left until daylight. They are several miles from Ketch Avery's hideout but they should be able to make it there by dawn.

The horses are drinking and Davey is standing a little way off, gazing up the valley, trying to make out the path ahead. The moon is a bright circle on the rippling water and the only sounds are the rilling of the stream and the soft breathing of the horses as they drink.

Ruby catches a flicker of movement in the corner of her eye.

"Davey!" she hisses

Several ragged clots of shadow start forward from the trees, long loping shadows that come on four legs. Ruby's blood runs cold; it is almost as if the wolves have been lying in wait for them. There are five of them, ranged in a line across the valley floor, cutting off any chance of escape into the trees. The horses scent the beasts and they turn, eyes wide, stamping in terror. Ruby grabs Caliban's mane and swings herself up into the saddle as Molly leaps away across the stream, sending a shower of moonsilvered spray up behind her.

In the space of a heartbeat, the wolves have covered half the distance from the trees. Dervish panics and rears up and Davey is almost dragged under her hooves as he struggles to keep hold of the reins. Ruby urges Caliban alongside the mare and reaches out for her bridle, steadying Dervish so that Davey can scramble up into the saddle.

"Ride for your life!" Ruby shouts, as Caliban wheels around and leaps after Molly.

The black stallion clears the stream in a single bound and gallops away up the path, with Davey and Dervish close behind.

The wolves halt at the water's edge, their hackles rising. The beasts snarl and speed off in pursuit along the opposite side of the stream.

The path is steep and narrow, with a sudden drop away to one side as it rises away from the steam bed. Ruby risks a glance back over her shoulder and sees that the wolves halting at a place where the stream narrows and falls into a deep cleft. The next instant, they have leapt the narrow gap, gaining the path behind the horses. Ruby does not need to urge Caliban on after that; he gallops up the narrow path in reckless terror. Molly appears suddenly ahead of them at the head of the valley, a dark silhouette outlined in silver against the sky.

The wolves run more easily on the slope than the horses and by the time Ruby and Davey have crested the rise the beasts are snapping at their horses heels, snarling and calling out to them in their unearthly voices. Ruby remembers the terror that froze her to the spot when she first met the wolves and pulls her mind free from the enchantment just in time. Caliban goes wild. He gives a fierce buck and tries to throw Ruby off but she holds tight.

"Turn your terror into speed!" she whispers into his ear. "They're no match for you on the flat ground - Run!"

    The path over the moor is clearly visible in the moonlight, a pale scar winding across the dark heather towards three outcrops of rock, rising against the moon like the squat figures of old men, their shoulders hunched against the wind; the Beggar Stones. This is the way to the high moor. Ruby glimpses Davey and Dervish not far behind. Dervish is spooked too but she is better trained than Caliban and she hasn't thrown Davey off.

    The riders race ahead, steadily gaining ground on the wolf pack. As they near the looming rocks their hopes of escaping begin to rise but as they pass the first of the stones two more wolves rise up from the heather, bounding forward and jumping up at the riders. Caliban leaps right over the lead wolf, striking it with his hoof as he goes, but Dervish is not so lucky. The second wolf catches her on the flank and she stumbles, sending Davey tumbling headlong into the heather. The chestnut mare is up again in an instant, shrieking with terror.

    Davey struggles to his feet. The wolves have halted a few feet away, sizing him up with their yellow eyes. They pad forward, their snouts low, their teeth glistening pale as bones in the moonlight. One of them growls, deep in its throat; the sound could almost be a cruel laugh. Davey casts about for something to defend himself with but there is nothing.

Davey hears the thunder of hooves behind him and turns to see Caliban bearing down on them. Ruby is crouched low in the saddle, her head against the stallion's neck. She can feel Caliban's terror of the wolves but stronger than that is his pride and his wild passion; he is born of warriors and there is a spark of dark fire in his heart that makes him rejoice in battle.

The wolves are taken by surprise at the sheer fury of the stallion's onslaught; one is trampled under his hooves and the other takes a savage blow to the back, leaping away with an eerie cry of pain, more human than wolf. Ruby brings the stallion about in a tight turn and gallops back toward Davey, who is already sprinting for the nearest of the Beggar stones.

With a start, Ruby sees that the other wolves have almost caught up with them. She pulls a pistol from her belt and points it back over her shoulder. The pack scatter as she fires and one wolf falls. She pulls a second loaded pistol free and urges Caliban forward. Up ahead, Davey has reached the stone and is beginning to climb. There is a ledge half way up and he pauses there, turning toward Ruby. She sees his eyes widen and he points away urgently over her shoulder but there is no time to turn and look. "Jump on behind!" she shouts, hoping that he can hear her over the thunder of Caliban's hooves. Ruby takes Caliban as close to the rock as she dares. She reins him in and Davey leaps on behind her. He lands squarely on the saddle but almost slips off as Caliban tries to rear up and throw him. Ruby clamps the stallion's flanks hard with her heels and pulls on the rein. Caliban snorts with rage but he keeps his hooves on the ground as Davey rights himself and grabs Ruby by the waist.

The shadow wolves are all around them now and as they gallop away from the Beggar stones the beasts close in. They surge forward on both sides, leaping all at once. Four wolves fall upon Caliban's left flank while the other two jump higher, knocking Ruby and Davey from the stallion's back. They fall together onto the heather as Caliban rears up, thrashing with his front legs. Ruby feels the earth tremble under the pounding of the stallion's hooves as he gallops away.

They lie on the heather, half stunned, bracing themselves for the onslaught of the Witch Wolves, but none comes. Ruby and Davey stumble to their feet, breathless and battered, to see all seven of the beasts pacing back and forth about them in a loose circle. They try to edge back toward the stones but the wolves close in, lunging forward, snapping their teeth and hounding them back onto the open ground.
"What are they doing?" hisses Davey. "Why don't they attack?"
"They have their orders."
Ruby and Davey wheel around at the sound of the voice. A tall figure steps out from behind the nearest stone, holding a cocked pistol in his hand.

Chapter 21.

Josia Colby meets Ruby's furious gaze with cold amusement.
"The wolves are your creatures," says Ruby.
"You are not the only one with secrets, Miss Gilbert."
"You can take your secrets to hell. From the looks of things you're more than half way there anyhow."
"I am not foolish enough to believe in such superstitious nonsense. There are no devils, nor gods, apart from those we create." The Squire nods toward the dark wolves. "I have some power in the summoning of demons, at least. Bones of beasts and souls of humans; The Witch Wolves are rather fearsome, aren't they?"
The wolves sit motionless, crouched in the heather, their yellow eyes trained upon Davey and Ruby.
"Is it true that you send your beasts to kidnap children and drink their blood?" asks Ruby.
The Squire laughs. "You make me sound like a monster." He lowers the pistol and steps closer, his voice softening. "Blood has potent magic in it. A cupful or so is not missed, even by a child." He shrugs. "Those who do not survive the ordeal would doubtless have perished anyway. Nature has no time for weaklings."

The quiet assurance with which the Squire speaks of his awful deeds chills Ruby's heart. He sees her fear. "You are an extraordinary young woman, Miss Gilbert. Until tonight, even I had not guessed that you were the infamous Jack Shadow."

As the Squire speaks, two figures emerge from the other side of the tall stone. Captain Ransome carries a hooded lantern in one hand and a drawn sword in the other, while Mr Furey holds a coil of rope and a club. The Squire's men halt a little way off, clearly wary of the wolves. Ruby's eyes remain fixed on Josia Colby - he is the real source of danger

If the Squire has the power to command dark magic, what chance do she and Davey stand against him? Ruby can feel the reassuring weight of the pistol in her belt. The handle is hidden by the folds of her cloak and the Squire seems not to have noticed it. They still have a chance, however desperate.

There comes the sound of galloping horses from the woods below.

"That will be the soldiers," muses the Squire. "Perhaps it is time for my pets to hide themselves. The Witch Wolves are veiled by charms enough, but it might be a little awkward if they were seen by a whole troop of men." The Squire opens his right hand and the Witch Wolves rise up as one, lifting their eyes to their master. He gives a whispered command and the beasts lope silently off into the night. "Stop skulking in the shadows and come tie these two up," the Squire calls out, gesturing Captain Ransome and Mr Furey forward with an impatient wave of his hand. "Kill them if they put up a struggle."

The Squire keeps his pistol trained on Ruby as the men approach. Captain Ransome places the lantern on the ground at his feet and sheathes his sword. He takes a length of rope from Mr Furey and steps forward to take hold of Davey.

Ruby pulls the pistol from her cloak and throws herself backwards, knocking Davey to the ground, out of range of the Squire's gun. Even as Ruby falls, the Squire raises his pistol to fire, but Captain Ransome's broad shoulders block his shot. On her feet again in a flash, Ruby kicks out at the lantern, sending it tumbling over. The glass shatters and a gout of flaming oil splatters out over the heather. The heather is tinder dry and it flares up at once, forcing Mr Furey to jump back smartly to avoid being set alight.
"Run Davey!" Ruby brandishes her pistol in Captain Ransome's face. "I'll be right behind you."
   The Squire steps to one side and levels his pistol at Ruby. Ruby raises her own gun and fires, the powder flash scorching along the side of Captain Ransome's arm as he lunges at her with his sword. The shot goes wide and Captain Ransome gives a bellow of pain. A split second later, the Squire fires his own pistol. Ruby feels the force of the bullet hitting her in the chest and she tumbles back, the breath gone from her lungs.
   The world is suddenly very still, the stars above her are bright and the sounds all about are sharp and clear. She hears a cry of pain from Davey and the sound of running feet. She hears the crackle of flames and the soft hiss of wind in the heather. She puts her hand up to her chest. There is no blood - no wound. Her hand finds the Kern on its silver chain. The shape of the bronze amulet has altered; one side of it is dented and the smooth metal is sharp against her fingertips - the Kern deflected the Squire's bullet!

Ruby takes a gasping breath. Her chest feels as if it has been split open with an axe but she is still alive! Wincing with pain, she rolls away over the heather and pushes herself to her feet. She looks up but the Squire is on her in an instant, grabbing her by the arm and pinning her down.

Davey runs to help Ruby but his path is blocked by Mr Furey. The rat-faced man swings his club and Davey ducks just in time to feel the billy club brush his scalp as it whips over his head. Davey twists away and stumbles through the burning heather. He feels something fall from the pocket of his coat; the book that Ruby gave him in Truro market. He's forgotten it was there.

At the sight of the book all of the Squire's composure falls away. He loosens his grip on Ruby's arm and lunges forward to where the book lies at the edge of the burning patch of heather.

It cannot be lost, so much rests on it!

Ruby told Davey about her discoveries at Colby Hall and he has read enough of the book to know what it contains. If even a portion of what is written there is true, then the Keys of Queen Mab would give awesome power to anyone able to use it. Davey sees how much Josia Colby wants the book and in the fierce clarity that can come in a moment of desperation, he sees an advantage to be gained. He grabs the book out of the fire and steps back.

Captain Ransome's sword cannot not reach Davey over the flames but he is keenly aware that Mr Furey is behind him somewhere in the darkness. He steps up to the blaze and holds the Keys of Queen Mab out over the flames.

"Let Ruby go free and call your men off or I will burn your book," says Davey.

Captain Ransome pauses, looking toward the Squire. He senses the tension in his master and sees how his eyes are fixed upon the book in Davey's hand. The Squire gives a curt nod to his henchman, instructing him to wait. From the corner of his eye Davey glimpses Mr Furey. He too has halted.

"I wonder why you place so much store by a collection of fairy tales?" says Davey. "It is almost as if you believe that Queen Mab is real."

"Queen Mab is as real as you or I - more real, perhaps; for she is immortal. The world is a far stranger and more perilous place that you know, Master Tachard, and there are worlds beyond this one that you cannot imagine." The Squire pulls Ruby up in front of him, bending her arm hard behind her back. "I have no time for this foolishness. If you wish to live to see the sun rise, you will bring the book to me now." The human voice is the first instrument of enchantment and there is a deep menace in the Squire's tone and a compelling authority that is hard to resist.

Ruby meets Davey's gaze, willing him to hold out. "You can have your foul book," says Davey. "Once you let Ruby go."

The Squire's eyes blaze but his face remains impassive. He summons all his will and checks his fury. There is no room for error. The boy is sharp enough and he has let his emotions betray him once.

He will not let his mask slip for a second time. "You have no chance, David. You are an accomplice to highway robbery and a fugitive from justice. You will go to the gallows if the troopers lay their hands on you. Give me the book and you have my word that I will do all that I can for you. I have the influence to protect you. It is your only chance. There is nothing else to bargain for."

Davey makes no reply, he feels himself wavering under the ferocity of the Squire's will but he draws strength from the defiant flame burning in Ruby's eyes. He steps closer to the fire.

"Let her go."

The Squire's face twists into a snarl.

"It seems that the schooling your father has lavished upon you has left no mark. You are as great a fool as he is." With surprising speed, the Squire draws a knife from his belt and presses it to Ruby's throat, pulling her arm tighter behind her until she cries out in pain. Davey's free hand clenches into a fist but he stands his ground. "I shall slit her throat if you do not hand me the book at once. My patience is quite run out."

"Stand firm, Davey, stand firm," Ruby mouths to him silently.

"If you harm her then your book will be lost forever," Davey replies, lowering the book nearer to the fire. A stray thread on his coat sleeve flares up in a hiss of flame and he catches the bitter whiff of burning cloth. The fire is blisteringly hot but he does not flinch. The Squire's jaw tightens.

Davey has no doubt that Josia Colby would kill them both as soon as blinking but it is becoming increasing clear just how much he wants the book. Sensing that he has the upper hand, Davey presses home his advantage. He drops his arm down to the level of the leaping flames and lets them scorch at the binding of the book.

"Your men will back away and you will put down the knife," Davey says, pulling his hand back from the fire.

With a gesture, the Squire motions Captain Ransome and Mr Furey back, his eyes not leaving Davey for an instant.

"Get over by the rock," Davey says.

With a glance at the Squire, the men do as he asks.

"Now the knife. Lower it."

The Squire takes the knife from Ruby's throat, though he keeps a firm hold on her arm.

Ruby's eyes widen in shock and she lifts her gaze to a spot just over Davey's right shoulder. For one heartstopping moment, Davey wonders if the Squire has stabbed Ruby in the back but then there comes a searing pain in his outstretched hand and he glimpses a swift, dark shape plunging past him into the fire.

The grey falcon catches the falling book in its talons and lifts up and away with a harsh cry of triumph. Squire Colby smiles and pushes Ruby to the ground at his feet.

"You will pay dearly for your impudence, Master Tachard."

Davey remains rooted to the spot. He sees the Squire advancing with the knife in his fist. He sees Ruby rise to her knees and catches a flurry of movement at the corner of his eye as Captain Ransome and Mr Furey run at him from the rock. The two men are only a few feet away when Ruby springs up and barges into them, tumbling Captain Ransome into the flames. Mr Furey falls too, lost from view behind the fire.
"Run Davey!" cries Ruby. She is pinned to the ground once more by the Squire. "They'll kill you for sure."
Captain Ransome has rolled through the flames and is roaring with rage as he beats at his burning coat. He throws off the coat and comes at Davey with his sword.
"Go!" says Ruby, her eyes blazing. "I can look after myself."
Davey is not about to leave her. He dodges under Captain Ransome's sword arm and runs toward Ruby and the Squire. The Squire has cast his knife aside as he struggles to control Ruby. Davey sees the bright glitter of the knife blade on the ground by the Squire's foot and lunges for it. He catches the knife up and turns toward Josia Colby but he has forgotten about Mr Furey. The lead weighted club crashes sickeningly into the side of Davey's head, rattling his teeth and sending him spinning away into darkness.

Chapter 22.

Davey opens his eyes to see stars. He feels the wind on his face and a throbbing pain in his head. He reaches up his fingers to find a lump on the side of his head the size of a hen's egg. He hears voices nearby and turns slowly to see the glimmer of a lantern, swaying to and fro. Two men are searching through the heather, arguing as they did so.
"Did you bring your shovel?" asks Mr Furey
"What for?"
"So we can dig a hole and chuck the boy in it."
"I didn't know we'd be digging any holes," mutters Captain Ransome, sulkily."Anyway, there's no sign of him. He must have got burned up in the fire."
"Then we'll have to dig a hole to put his bones in, won't we?" Mr Furey stops and sniffs the air.
"A burning body smells a lot like roast pork. Do you smell pork, Ransome?"
"Don't talk about pork, I'm famished. I haven't had a bite of scran all night."
"Shine the glim over here - I see something."
"You should have cut his throat when you had the chance," says Captain Ransome, swinging the light over the ground at Mr Furey's feet.
"That little vixen was putting up such a fight that it took all three of us to tie her up."
"We should have killed her too."
"I'd have liked that," says Mr Furey with a smile. "But the Squire has other ideas."
"What's he want with her?"

"She'll not bother us again. Her pretty face will be decorating the Gallows Tree before long."
The men are gradually working their way towards the place where Davey lies, Mr Furey bending over to examine the ground and Captain Ransome coming along beside him with the lantern.
"I don't see him," says the big man. "I bet he's legged it."
"If he's run off, then the Squire's pets will catch up with him."
The men are only a few paces away from Davey but they have their backs to him for the moment
This might be his only chance to escape.

Davey rises slowly to his feet and begins to step away across the heather. He has only taken a few paces when he treads on a dry twig.
"There he is!" bellows Captain Ransome.
Davey sprints away. His head stabs with pain at the sudden exertion but he ignores it. He hears the sounds of the two men crashing over the heather behind him and puts everything else from his mind.

A sudden gully opens at Davey's feet and he leaps over it, clearing the stream and landing on the far side. The loose bank collapses under his weight but he scrambles up and runs on. A moment later there is a splash followed by a yelp of pain. There is another splash and a bellow of rage as Captain Ransome follows Mr Furey, head first, into the ditch.
"I'll throttle you!" yells Mr Furey. He falls back again with a cry of agony, his ankle twisted. "Get after the little rat," he hisses at Captain Ransome, who is

lumbering up out of the stream, wiping mud from his eyes.
"It'll go worse for you if I have to drag you back!" shouts Captain Ransome.

The moor stretches emptily ahead, miles of heather and rock with nowhere to hide. Davey's only hope is to get to the forest, half a mile away down the hillside. Mist is rising among the trees, which will make good cover. Davey turns down the hill, following the course of the stream.

The stream bed soon deepens into a gully and Davey jumps down to run in the ankle deep water. It is slippery underfoot but he feels safer there, hidden from view by the rising walls of the gully.

On a good day, Davey could easily outrun Captain Ransome - but this is not a good day; he is already at the limit of his endurance, his head throbs with pain and his legs are like jelly. He can hear Captain Ransome's splashing footfalls drawing closer. There is no way up the slippery walls; the only thing to do is to keep on running.

A shout echoes out:
"When I catch hold of you - I'm going to rip out your gizzard!"
Davey pushes on, using every last ounce of his strength, leaping recklessly over the wet stones, slipping and stumbling against the rocky walls. His lungs are burning and he is starting to feel dizzy. It is hard to judge how far he has come down the hill, but he must be near the forest by now; the stream bed is flattening out.

Davey turns a corner and skids to a halt, catching himself on a rock only just in time stop himself from falling headlong into the stream. The edge of the forest is in sight now, a hundred yards further on, but standing between him and the trees, on the far side of the stream, is a wolf.

The wolf raises its head from the stream and stares at Davey with its pale eyes. The creature is as huge as the Squire's servants but its fur is silvery grey and its eyes are the colour of smoke.

The beast is only a few paces away across the water and Davey can see the mist of its breath and bright droplets of water clinging to the soft fur at its muzzle. There is something reassuring about this; Davey finds it hard to imagine the Witch Wolves doing anything as ordinary as drinking from a stream. As he returns the grey wolf's gaze, Davey realises that he was not afraid; the wolf is not a menacing presence. For all its great size and savage appearance, the wolf's eyes seem sad, like those of a lost creature, far from home.

Captain Ransome rounds the corner. He smiles nastily and draws his sword, too intent upon Davey to notice the wolf on the other side of the stream.
"Time to sort you out, once and for all -" he begins, but he is cut off by a deep growl from the wolf. Captain Ransome turns to see the wolf take a purposeful step forward, the fur at its shoulders rising in a stiff ruff.
"You just stay back," says Captain Ransome, pointing his sword at the wolf and swallowing nervously.

"You're the Squire's beast and I'm the Squire's man - so we're both on the same side, ain't we?"
But the wolf is not the Squire's creature, and it has no liking for Captain Ransome. It gives another growl and springs toward him over the moonsilvered water. This is too much for Captain Ransome, who turns and runs back up the canyon as fast as his legs can carry him. The wolf bounds after the running man, passing so close to Davey that he feels the soft swish of its fur on his face as it goes.

Davey kneels by the stream, bewildered and amazed. From the canyon, he hears the echo of Captain Ransome's running footsteps, then a snarl, a scream and a chilling silence. Davey is on his feet in an instant, running for the trees.

A mile or so into the wood, Davey stumbles across a cave, the entrance half hidden behind a thicket of rowan trees. Without a second thought, he crawls inside and lets himself down gently onto a drift of dry leaves. Aching and exhausted, he falls asleep at once.

Chapter 23.

Ruby shivers awake. She is lying on a stone floor in a narrow cell. The only light is a tiny window high up in the wall. Her chest hurts each time she breathes and there is a dark bruise on her breast bone, shaped like a horse. She takes out the Kern and holds it up to the light. The Squire's bullet struck the amulet squarely in the middle, making a round dent and bending the horse out of shape.

"You have brought me luck so far," Ruby whispers. "I hope it's not all gone."

Ruby climbs stiffly to her feet and begins to pace the floor, trying to make sense of what happened; she remembers seeing Davey go down under Mr Furey's club and fighting her way out of the Squire's grasp to get to him. Someone must have knocked her out after that - probably Captain Ransome. She dimly recalls being tied up and thrown over the back of a horse. The soldiers didn't carry her far, so she is most likely at Colby Hall, or in the jail in the village. Either way, her position is hopeless; the Squire knows her secret and is only a matter of time before it is all over.

The cell holds nothing but a cracked jug and a crust of bread. The water in the jug is sour and the bread is worm-eaten. The cell door is of heavy oak, bound with iron and locked fast. Ruby pounds on it with her fists and calls out but no-one comes in answer.

The sun chinks through the clouds sending bright bars of golden light across the wall of the cell but it does little to raise Ruby's spirits. She sits down with her back to the door and lets her head rest on her knees.

A soft sound brings Ruby out of her despair. Something moves at the window; a bird, bobbing about between the bars. She breaks the bread into crumbs and tosses a handful up onto the window ledge. The sparrow hops forward to the edge of the sill and peers down into the cell. After a moment's hesitation, he spreads his wings and flies down to land in the patch of sunlight at Ruby's feet. She breaks more bread for him, watching the way the light catches in his feathers. They are dusty grey at the bird's breast, with russet and chestnut, barred with black, along the wings and back. She remembers the sunny morning, just a few days ago, when she freed a sparrow caught in the hedge. So much has happened since then. Could this be the same bird? She smiles.

"You'll need to find another friend, little one. I am no use to anyone now."

The sparrow hops closer and cheeps at Ruby. She breaks off more crumbs and tosses them onto the floor.

When the sparrow has eaten his fill he spreads his wings and takes a turn about the cell, before disappearing through the high window.

The sparrow's visit has eased Ruby's heart a little and she moves to sit against the wall, letting the warm sunlight fall on her face.

It is well into the morning before the sun has risen high enough to reach down through the trees into the cave where Davey sleeps. He opens his eyes and lies still for some while, dazed and confused, breathing in the scent of dry leaves and wet earth. When he tries to move, he finds that his whole body aches like one enormous bruise; his head jabs with pain, his shoulder is stiff, his burned hand stings and there is a deep gash on the back of the other hand, where the falcon's talons cut him.

The sound of splashing water nearby makes Davey aware of how thirsty he is. He rolls to his knees and turns toward the sunlight. That's when he sees the girl, sitting in the shadows on the other side of the cave entrance.

"Where the devil did you come from?" asks Davey, stepping back in surprise and bashing his head on the low roof of the cave. "Ouch!" The girl blinks and shrinks back against the wall at the sound of his voice, clearly terrified. "It's alright," says Davey, rubbing his head and speaking more gently. "I won't hurt you. I just got a bit of a fright."

The girl says nothing.

She looks about his own age and in a desperate state. Her dress is in tatters, her hair is tangled and her face, under the thick layer of dirt, is pale. What is she doing out here alone on the moor? For a moment, Davey quite forgets about his own problems.

"I'm Davey," he says. "Who are you?"

"Lucy," she replies. She bites her lip and stares at him warily, clearly trying to decide if he is to be trusted. "I've been hiding. I didn't see you when I came in."

"Who are you hiding from?"
"I ran away from Colby Hall."
"I can understand that."
Lucy shakes her head.
"You don't know the half of it." She buries her head in her hands and begins to sob. "I just want to go home to my Grannie in Penzance!"

When Lucy has stopped crying Davey gives her his handkerchief.
"Tell me what happened," he says.
"You won't believe me."
"Try me."

Lucy Cotton tells Davey how she stumbled into the tower room in the abandoned wing of the Colby Hall: "The Squire grabbed me from behind and tied me up. Then he cut my hand open and caught my blood in bowl. He mixed it up with something and made me drink it." Lucy shudders at the memory."He was shouting strange words and there were shadows creeping and howling around the room, shadows with teeth and nasty yellow eyes.

"I'm not sure what happened after that - not until I saw the moonlight. It was so bright and lovely, if felt like I'd never seen anything so beautiful . . ."
Lucy pauses for breath. Telling her story has brought some colour back to her cheeks.

"I don't remember much of anything that's happened since the Squire gave me that horrid drink - I think it did something to me. I'm alright in the daytime but when I fall asleep I have nightmares and I wake up miles away. I suppose I must go walking in

my sleep." Lucy glares at Davey, half defiant, half scared. "You probably think I'm crazy."
Davey shakes his head.
"The Squire's in league with the Devil," says Lucy."He's a sorcerer like his father."

Now that he has found her, Davey can't leave Lucy alone on the moor. She is scared out of her wits and she needs to be somewhere safe. The only person who Davey can think of turning to for help is Farmer Finch. Davey trusts him and, like most folk in Bascome valley, he has little love for Squire Colby. Even if Finch can't help him find Ruby, he will be able to look after Lucy.

Davey gives Lucy his jacket and, after they have drunk at the stream, he leads them off in the direction of Bascome.

It is mid afternoon by the time they reach Finch's farm. Lucy is asleep on her feet by then and Mrs Finch takes one look at her and sends her straight off to bed.
"There's a story at the back of all this, I'll wager," says Farmer Finch.
"I'm in more trouble than I can explain," says Davey.
Finch raises an eyebrow.
"It's the talk of the county that Seth and Tom Gilbert were broken out of the jail last night by Jack Shadow." When Davey makes no reply Finch goes on. "I don't have you down for a highwayman, Davey. Young Tom's got the fire in his guts but not the wits, and Seth is a blindman, so?"

"It's probably best if I don't tell you any more," says Davey.

Finch nods "Seth Gilbert is as true a man as I've ever met and we go back a long way. I'll do whatever I can for him and his kin."

"Can you get word to Ketch Avery and tell him that Tom and Seth are at his hideout near the Pikestone? They need his help. I have to find out what's happened to Ruby."

"I can tell you that myself. She's in the jailhouse in Bascome and I have heard there's to be a trial tomorrow."

"Tomorrow! That's too soon."

"Squire Colby is the Magistrate, Davey, and with a whole company of troopers at his command the Squire can make the law as he wishes in Bascome Valley."

"We must rescue her!" says Davey, leaping to his feet.

Finch shakes his head.

"I'd like to help Ruby as much as you would but after what happened with Seth and Tom she's guarded by so many soldiers that you'd need an army to break her out of there." Sam Finch puts his large hand on Davey's shoulder, his weather beaten face lined with concern. "Ruby's beyond our help now. You'd serve her best by doing all you can for Seth and Tom. They'll need all the friends they can get before all this is played out."

"I'll not let Ruby die on the rope," says Davey. He flings off Finch's hand and makes for the door.

"Whoa there!" Sam calls after him. "If you're mad enough to throw yourself away after rescuing Ruby then at least let me help you."

A little while later, Davey is creeping along the hedgerows toward the village. He has swapped his clothes for some old ones of Farmer Finch's; muddy boots, a ragged jacket and a weather stained hat pulled over his face gave him the look of a farmer's boy. The disguise won't fool anyone who knows him but it will keep him safe from the troopers. Davey has no clear plan, other than to find out all he can about Ruby's whereabouts and try, somehow, to free her before the morning. The outcome of the trial is a forgone conclusion - he knows that.

Davey manages to keep out of sight behind the hedges as far as the bridge. The road seems quiet and Davey decides to chance his luck.
Two soldiers come riding down the main street just as Davey passes the inn and he has to step into a doorway to let them go by. They pass without giving him a glance and he heads on up the hill. He sees more soldiers, gathered in a group in the village square, their red coats bright against the whitewashed walls of the cottages. He steps away down an alley and slips along behind the garden walls until he reaches the back of his father's house. He's taking a great risk going there but he has a feeling that he will be leaving Bascome soon, perhaps forever, and there are some things that he wants to take with him.

Davey climbs the wall and in through his bedroom window. He creeps softly to the door and listens. The house is silent save for the ticking of a clock in the hallway. He jams a chair under the doorknob turns to his writing desk. He pauses at the sight of his books; will he ever see them again? He is an outlaw now and there is no knowing what his life will be like. Davey takes out a pen and a sheaf of paper and begins to write

The letter seems an inadequate thing when he has finished it but there is no time for anything else. As he folds the paper, Davey does his best to push aside the image of his mother's anguished expression as she reads it.

There comes a sudden hammering at the front door of the vicarage and Davey starts up in alarm, spilling the ink bottle over the desk. He lifts the letter free just in time and throws it onto the bed, then steps to the door to listen. He hears the maid's voice, then his father's and then another voice that sends a shiver of panic down his spine.

"Have you seen your son, Reverend?" asks the Squire."There are urgent matters I must discuss with him."

"I have not seen David at all today," the Reverend Tachard replies." The lad was not in his bed last night. To tell the truth, I am rather concerned for his welfare."

"You would do well to be concerned," says the Squire. "You must let me know at once if he returns."

"If he returns? What do you mean by that?"

"I mean, Reverend, that your son is in a good deal of trouble and his only hope is to give himself up to my mercy. I can help him, but only if he will help me. Be sure to tell him that."

"Speak more plainly, sir. What kind of trouble has David come to?"

Davey is surprised to hear genuine concern in his father's voice.

"I have reason to believe that David has got himself mixed up with the Gilbert gang. There are reports that he had a hand in their escape from jail."

"David is an honest boy," replies the Reverend Tachard firmly. "He would not consort with criminals. Josia, I am shocked that you would suggest such a thing."

The Squire snorts.

"David would not be the first young man who fell into crime on account of a pretty girl and he would do well to come forward of his own free will. It will go ill for him if he is caught by the troopers."

"This is pure foolishness."

Davey feels a pang of remorse as the Reverend speaks up for him. The old man has showed Davey little kindness recently but he is still his father.

"Let me know if you see him," growls the Squire. "For both your sakes."

Davey hears the Squire's heavy footsteps in the hall and the loud report of the front door slamming shut behind him. He expects to hear his father come up the stairs but after some muffled talk in the hall the study door closes once more and there is silence.

For a moment Davey considers going to his father and telling him everything. But he decides it would do no good. The concern that he heard in his father's voice does not mean that he is a changed man and once he knows the truth about Ruby the Reverend would side with the Squire.

Davey is on his own.

Davey steps back to the window. Taking out a sheet of blotting paper he dries the spilled ink and places the letter in the middle of the desk where it will not be missed. Then he takes his journal and a folio of poems from the shelf. As Davey makes to stow the books away in his satchel, a paper slips out from between the pages of the journal. It is a section that he copied from Ruby's book as he sat under the oak in Truro market place. Was that really only yesterday afternoon? It seems a whole lifetime ago.

Davey holds the paper up to the light:

"For the summoning of a Faery Helper
The charm is simple enough to cast, but should not be undertaken lightly. The sprite summoned may be of a capricious nature and one must choose one's commands with great care. To perform the charm, all one must do is repeat the words of the spell with full intention to succeed."

Below the brief instructions is one of the curious rhymes that had so fascinated Davey. He gazes at the words, letting the sounds of the arcane language move on his tongue. The language has a curious music to it, something at once beautiful and troubling. The meanings of the words seem to come to Davey as he speaks them and pass away as the sounds fade.

"Calathon alata'bey darkesta,
 Calata celesta cassaita,
 Destinat amiana ak'serphias,
 Darkeste at'orphorea a'sidhais."

When the spell is done there comes a silence so profound that it seems as if the whole world has fallen still to listen - all except Davey's heart, which thunders like a drum in his ears.

   The sound of a shutter slamming in the wind brings Davey to his senses. He shakes himself and puts the paper down, feeling rather foolish. Things are truly desperate if he is willing to resort to believing in hokum like that. The Squire might claim to be a sorcerer but what does that mean? He has a pack of trained wolves who obey his will and he has terrified a kitchen maid into believing that he can summon the devil. There is no mystery to it; the Squire is a ruthless man who inspires fear in those about him. Ridiculous notions about Faery magic will bring Davey no closer to rescuing Ruby. He sits back down on the bed, disconsolate.
   What should he do next? He has seen the troopers in the town square, no doubt sent there to guard Ruby. Farmer Finch was right, there is nothing that Davey can hope to do on his own. Seth and Tom

might help but first he must find Ketch Avery's hideout on the moor.

Chapter 24.

The clatter of boots outside the door of her cell jerks Ruby to her feet. A key scrapes in the lock and the door is opened to reveal a soldier with a drawn sword in his hand. He scowls at her warily and withdraws to allow a tall man to enter.

 Josia Colby dismisses the soldier with a curt nod of his head and the door is closed behind him.

"You have been an astonishing amount of trouble to me, Miss Gilbert," says the Squire.

Ruby makes no reply.

The light from the barred window falls across the Squire's shoulder and face in bright strips, dazzling him. He lifts his hand to shade his eyes and steps to one side so that he can see Ruby more clearly in the dimness of the cell.

"I told you once before that I admire a girl with spirit," he says." But I wonder if you have the wisdom to know when to stop fighting against your fate?"

"Fate is what you make of it," says Ruby. She had meant to keep from speaking a single word but her anger gets the better of her.

"You are caught. Your father and brother are on the run, soon to join you, while the Reverend's wayward son has shown himself to be a gutless coward. There is no one to help you now but yourself."

Seth and Tom must still be free! Ruby keeps her face blank, hiding the relief that she feels. She wants badly to ask about Davey but she holds back.

"Your trial is set for this afternoon but I do not think that there will be many witnesses to defend you. It would be a mortal waste for you to hang."

"I am not afraid to die."

"Perhaps not, but who will look after your little sister when you are gone? The workhouse is such an ugly place."

Ruby clenches her fists. This man has been the ruin of her life, one way or another. Now he dares to threaten Katy!

"You could make it very easy for yourself," the Squire says, his voice softening.

As she holds the Squire's gaze, Ruby feels a heaviness wash over her. His eyes open out into two wells of darkness into which she feels herself falling. She stumbles, reaching out a hand to the wall to steady herself.

The Squire has long ago perfected the power of his voice to work upon the minds of others and he puts forth all his art and speaks in tones most beguiling: "There is no reason for you to stay here, and no reason for you to die on the hangman's rope. If you were to agree to come and live at Colby Hall, then you could walk free at once. You would be safe there. You would have all that you could ever want and then, perhaps, when you are old enough, you might become my wife. I have the power, not only to release you from this jail but to set you free from your poverty."

Perhaps it would be best if she just did as he asked? She could marry him - it would be an easy enough thing to do. Would it be worse than death? And Katy, at least, deserves the chance of something better. Living at the Manor would not be all that bad and Josia could not watch her always; she would find a way to escape and she could take Katy with her, send word to Seth and Tom and make a new life somewhere far away.

"It is only you and I, and that foolish boy, David Tachard, who know the truth about Jack Shadow. No one else need ever find out," continues the Squire. He speaks of Davey as if he were alive. That is good. Ruby nods her head. Her weariness is growing stronger and she feels as if she wants nothing more than to curl up somewhere warm and sleep for a very long time. What the Squire says makes sense; he is offering her a way out of the mess that she has created and she would be a fool not to take it.

Josia Colby senses that Ruby is weakening and he reaches out to her. She lets him take her arm and does not notice the bracelet of spidersilk and human hair that he slips over her wrist.

"You look so very like her," the Squire says, his voice no more than a whisper.

"Like who?" Ruby asks sleepily.

"Catherine Sharpe."

"You knew her?" Ruby frowns. Surely her grandmother had died before Josia Colby had been born? Ruby's thoughts are becoming muddled and she is too drowsy to notice the unearthly look that has come into the Squire's eyes; a look of longing and of madness. In the dim light of the cell the Squire's face seems suddenly to age and his broad shoulders to stoop.

Ruby is falling under the power of the Heartbinding Charm and all that is needed is for him to pull tight the final thread - once Ruby has submitted to a betrayal then she will be utterly caught.
"All you need do is give up your father and brother," the Squire says quietly, managing to make his voice sound almost sorrowful. "You will be saving them from a trooper's bullet by turning them in and you have my word of honour that they will be spared from the gallows. Life in the Americas is not so bad. The work is no harder than here. Indeed, there are those who go to the colonies as convicts and, by honest toil, are redeemed and return home as made men."
Ruby feels faintness wash over her. Just tell him where they are and have done with it.

Ruby feels something else then, a soft presence that steadies her. She remembers the touch of another hand; her mother stroking her cheek. She hears a gentle voice in her ear.
" Stay true to your heart, Ruby, stay true and you will always find your way."
A sudden tremor shakes Ruby's body, bringing her suddenly to her senses. She throws off the Squire's hand and steps away from him. She feels something biting at her wrist and her fingers find the bracelet of silk and hair, pulling it off without a second thought.
"I will not betray my kin and I will never submit to be your wife!" Ruby says, her eyes blazing.
"Do not make the same mistake that she did," the Squire says, gripping hard to Ruby's arm and pulling her toward him again. "Catherine was proud and I loved her for that - but she passed to dust in the end."

Ruby gasps as she sees the changed look of the Squire. His face is that of a man a hundred years old; his hair white, his skin drawn tight over the bones of his skull, his deep set eyes burning with a terrible hunger. Tearing her sleeve from his grasp, Ruby struggles free and falls back against the wall. The vision lasted for only for the space of a heartbeat but in that instant Ruby knew that she was seeing the true face of Squire Colby.

The Squire nods, as if reading her thoughts.

"You are not the only one with secrets," the Squire says with a smile. His face is young once more but the madness still smoulders in his eyes. "I shall tell you all there is to know. You will understand my power then, and if it does not change your mind, you will die.

"It was the hope of enchanting Catherine Sharpe that led me to begin dabbling in witchcraft. Of course, I soon learned that most of what people call magic is mere trickery and superstition but, here and there, I found hints of genuine power amid all the hokum. Little by little, I learned the arts of Sorcery and Necromancy, the arts of Summoning and Binding. I even gleaned some scraps of Faery Magic.

"I was in my hundredth year, and near to death, when I discovered the formula for the Elixir in a fragment from the lost book of Queen Mab." The Squire holds Ruby's gaze and smiles. "I think that you know the spell I speak of?"

Ruby remembers the words that she read in the tower room at Colby hall and shudders.

"The making of the Elixir would have daunted a lesser man," says the Squire. "Even I had misgivings about drinking such a deadly draft. In the end, only the certainty of my coming death gave me the courage to take it.

As soon as I had drunk the Elixir, I felt my heart cease beating. I lay in darkness, dead to the world. I felt my body corrupt and rot and my bones crumble. But though my body fell to dust, my spirit endured, wracked with unimaginable pain.

Just as the suffering became so great that I thought I could bear no more, there came a fresh torture; needles of fire ran through my being as my body began to grow anew. Like a butterfly in a cocoon I struggled, screaming with the agony of rebirth.

Imagine my joy when, at last, I woke and I was young again! I was still weak from the ordeal but I could feel the power of my body returning by the hour. When I called the servant who had kept watch over my chamber the wretch fell to his knees at the sight of me. I plunged a dagger into his to keep my secret hidden!" The Squire laughs, his eyes sparking with crazed intensity.

Ruby's mind is reeling; the Squire is clearly insane - he must be?

"I put the poor fool's body into the coffin that had been prepared for me and had him buried in my place in the family tomb, but there was an unforeseen problem; I had not considered that the spell would work quite so well. I was young again but who would believe that I was Nathaniel Colby? And if they did believe, what would they do? Already my greedy relatives were scheming to get their hands on my fortune.

The signature of a crooked lawyer and a forged will were all it took to invent for myself a long lost son. Thus, old Nathaniel died and I become my own son, Josia Colby." The Squire smiles and Ruby knows, with cold certainty, that all he's told her is true.

"Catherine Sharpe was long dead by then but with the Elixir I hoped to bring her back. I exhumed her bones and performed the spells but the Elixir only works upon living flesh. The bodies of the dead cannot be remade so easily." The Squire pauses and when he speaks again it is in a whisper." I remember her cracked voice laughing at me from the empty mouth of her skull. Even in death she spurned me."

The Squire grips Ruby by the arm and brings his face to hers. "You are so like her, in body and in spirit - proud and beautiful. It is almost as if she had been reborn - just as I have been reborn!"

"I have the complete Keys of Queen Mab now and soon there will be no more need of the Elixir. Immortality and the command of men and spirits will be mine. There will be no one on earth to stand against me! You could share in that, Ruby. You could be an immortal. You could be a goddess, as beautiful and eternal as the Faerie Queen herself!"
The Squire reads the terror in Ruby's eyes and releases her.

"Your father and brother would be saved - I could pardon them with a single stroke of my pen. All you need do is become mine. I could make you my slave in a moment. But I have enough servants. You must come of your own free will."

The Squire has cast no enchantment upon Ruby this time. Instead, he has spread the truth before her, in all its terror and wonder. If she agrees to go with him then the lives of all those she loves will be spared. Once more, Ruby pauses; she thinks of Katy, of Tom and Seth. Her own fate is of little consequence - but to marry such a monster? To join him in his madness? She hears the voice again, faraway and soft as thistledown:

"Stay true to your heart, Ruby, Stay true. "

"I have given you my answer," says Ruby."I would rather die than become your wife."

The Squire makes to grab her and Ruby spits into his face. He stops in his tracks and Ruby prepares herself for a blow. None comes; the Squire simply turns away and wipes his face on his coat sleeve.

By the time Squire Colby raises his eyes, the crazed look has passed. He stands tall again and his face is pitiless. His gaze falls upon the Kern. The amulet has slipped free of Ruby's dress in the struggle and it hangs free on its chain, glimmering like dull gold in the dimness of the cell.

"I first saw that amulet at Catherine's throat," says the Squire softly. "But I had no idea of its power then." Ruby takes the Kern in her hand and steps back against the wall. The Squire smiles. "Do not worry. The magic of the Kern is capricious. If I took it from you it by force then it would be of no use to me. It only retains its power if it is freely given."

Ruby holds the Squire's gaze. He clearly wants the Kern. That might give her some advantage - if only she could work out how to use it?

"The Kern is such an ugly, worn out thing," says the Squire. "And yet your mother died to keep it."

"What do you mean?"

"Do you think that your mother died of a fever?" The Squire laughs and Ruby's blood turns to ice at the sound of it. "I tried to bargain with her but she would not see reason. I offered to let her keep her life and her freedom, I offered her gold, I even promised to give your father his job back."

"In exchange for what?"

"For the promise of your hand in marriage, once you came of age, and for the Kern, of course."

"What did you do to my mother?" asks Ruby in a choked whisper.

"Taking a human life by sorcery is not difficult," says the Squire. There is an exaltation in his eyes, as if he feels a sense of twisted pride in what he has done "Your mother put too much faith in love. Love makes us weak, it makes us vulnerable to fear and through fear a whole life can be unraveled."

Ruby stands as still as a stone, her rage at the Squire hardening into cold hatred, sharp and deadly as a steel blade. She considers the possibility of leaping at him and taking his throat in her hands, but she knows that he is too strong for her. Perhaps she should agree to marry him, after all - she could go along with the pretence until he drops his guard and then kill him in his sleep? She weighs the idea in her mind; could she endure such a thing?

No.

She must find another way. She has to keep him talking.

"What do you want the Kern for?"

"What you hold is no mere luck charm, Ruby; it is a key to the gates of Faerie. If you had bothered to read the book that you stole from me, then you would know that."

For all his power, the Squire is a fool, and he is wrong about her mother. She wasn't weak. Lizzie Gilbert was strong in ways that Squire Colby could never understand. The love that Squire despises was what made her strong and that love is with Ruby still; she feels its presence all around her.

"You will have neither me nor the Kern," says Ruby.

The Squire shrugs.

"The tales do not tell what happens to the Kern if its owner dies; its power may be lost, but it does not matter. There are other ways to travel into Mab's kingdom."

Ruby feels the full force of the Squire's mesmeric will bear down upon her but it slides off her now like water from a stone.

"Agreeing to marry me is your only chance to live," he says. "Will you consent?"

"I will not."

"So be it. You will hang in the morning and your family will hang with you. A blind man and a half witted boy will not evade capture for long."

Ruby stands staring after the Squire until the door of the cell has slammed behind him and his footsteps

have faded down the corridor. Then she sinks to her knees, shaken to the core by all she has heard. She holds tightly to the Kern and closes her eyes.
"If there is any power in you - then help me! " she whispers.

Chapter 25.

The light on the leaded window pane is dimming toward dusk, painting the room with an eerie, watergreen radiance. The bird song echoes strangely and the walls seem half dissolved in pooling shadows.

The man is silhouetted against the glow of the window. He has taken the chair from the door and sits, balanced rather precariously on two legs, with his boots up on Davey's desk. He has Davey's open folio of poems upon his knees and holds a sheet of manuscript in his hand, which he studies with great interest.

The man is slightly built, clean shaven, with curly brown hair falling loose at his neck. He wears an elegant coat of dark blue silk, brown leather britches and long, black boots. His face is delicate and feline, with a thin lipped mouth and high cheekbones, and his skin is very pale. He appears youthful but there is something about the man's stillness and poise that speak of much greater experience. The colour of his mischievous, twinkling eyes is impossible to fathom.

Davey wakes fully with a start; the day is almost gone - how could he possibly have fallen asleep? He might have been discovered at any moment! He jumps to his feet and the curious man, who Davey had at first taken to be a figment of his dream, turns to him and smiles. It is an unsettling smile; impudent and dangerous.

"You are awake," says the blue-coated man. His voice is clear and high, with an unfamiliar, lilting accent

"How did you get in here?" stammers Davey.
The man lowers the manuscript.
"I came via the stairs, though I could doubtless have arrived in a more impressive fashion. Would that please you in future?"
Davey stands blinking at the strange visitor, completely unable to get his bearings. Is he still dreaming? The boards under his feet feel solid enough. On the desk the empty bottle of ink lies where he had placed it, on top of the letter to his parents. Davey passes his hand across his face.

The blue-coated man seems quite relaxed. He leans back a little further on the chair and stretches like a cat. He offers no obvious threat but neither does his presence give Davey any sense of comfort.
"Are you sent by the Squire? asks Davey
"I am not sent at all but, rather, called upon," the man says, his eyes amused. He seems to be enjoying Davey's confusion. "You spoke the words of command and I came. It was a little rude, I thought, for you to be asleep upon my arrival, but I have found diversion in these lines of yours - some of them are rather good. " He tosses Davey's poems carelessly onto the desk."They would please my Queen. She loves poets above all things."
"Are you a Spaniard ?"
The man raises an eyebrow.
"I have seen the Queen of Spain and I can tell you that the rumours of Isabella's beauty are rather overdone. Her eyebrows are too close together and she has the manners of peasant." Davey blinks and makes no reply. The man sighs and shakes his head.

"I am not a Spaniard, Master Tachard, I am from another land, one much nearer at hand, but far harder to reach, and the Queen of whom I speak is no pale mortal girl. My sovereign is her radiant highness Queen Mab, the Lady of the Seven Stars, the most beloved of all the Sidhe, "

At the mention of Queen Mab, Davey feels an icy tingle of fear rise up his spine.

"Who are you?"

The blue coated man jumps nimbly to his feet and bows low.

"I am Perian," he says. "And, by the binding power of the spell that called me here, I am disposed to be at your service, David Tachard. Provided, of course, that we can come to amicable terms." The man winks cheekily at this point, but there is a sudden steel in his eyes that makes Davey wary.

"Terms?"

"Of course, summoning me is not enough; a bargain of some sort is required."

Davey frowns, quite at a loss.

"How do you know my name?"

"The same way that I know my own," replies the man, infuriatingly." You are the one who called me, after all."

Davey glances nervously toward the door. In his surprise at encountering the curious man he has quite forgotten the danger of the situation. Their voices will easily be heard downstairs and it is only a matter of time before someone comes to investigate.

"There is no need to worry," says Perian, seeming to read Davey's thoughts." I have put a Glamour upon the whole house. Your mother is dreaming happily over her needlepoint by the parlour window, while the Reverend Tachard slumbers over his sermon and the maid snores away in the pantry, with her face in the butter. We shall not be disturbed."

The little man seems very pleased with himself. He steps back to sit at the desk, watching Davey all the while with his unsettling eyes. On the desk stands a small oil painting in a wooden frame, showing a sailing ship under a stormy sky. As Perian passes close to it, the painted sea shimmers, the boat's sail trembles and the clouds begin to tumble. At the edge of his senses, Davey catches the sound of crying gulls and the scent of salt on the wind.

"Are you a magician?" he asks.

Perian laughs. It is a wild and troubling laugh and Davey wonders for a moment if the man is quite mad. "I am no magician," he says." I have some skill of Glamour, enough for my small wants, but no great craft. The price of that is too high, as you should be quite aware." The little man narrows his eyes and studies Davey shrewdly. "You seem no more than a boy. I wonder where you came across such a potent spell? Summoning me is not an easy thing to do."

Davey's eyes flick involuntarily toward the pile of papers on the desk. The rhyme that he copied from the Squire's book lies there among his poems. The knowing look in Perian's eye tells him that he has seen it already but Davey's instincts warn him against telling the visitor any more.

"I had thought that the few books where such magic might be found had been destroyed long ago," continues Perian. "Indeed, I lit the fire underneath them myself and saw the printing press destroyed. I do not like to be summoned by mortals."

"What are you?" Davey asks, looking Perian in the eye as boldly as he can manage.

"That would depend on who you were to ask. I have been called many things in my time; a messenger, a deceiver, a thief and a faithful servant, to name but a few. Your father would most likely tell you that I am the Devil." Perian grins, showing a mouth full of very white, sharp looking teeth. Davey notices the man's ears then, half hidden by his curling hair. They are small and delicately pointed and seem to be covered in a down of soft, brown fur.

"Are you the devil?" asked Davey.

This seems to amuse Perian very much.

"I have never met the gentleman in question," he laughs." You mortals, on the other hand, speak of him so often that I imagine you must know him well." Perian narrows his eyes and gives Davey a look that manages to be both mocking and deeply thoughtful at the same time. "It seems to me, that the Devil lives only in the hearts of men and I am certainly not a man. Of course, if I were Old Nick, then I would doubtless spin you just such a tale. He is a famous trickster, is he not?"

"You are a Faery?"

"If you like," says Perian softly. "I am the personal servant of Queen Mab, the ruler of the Twilight Land. I am her messenger and I fly the length of the Nine Worlds at her bidding. The gates of Dream and Death stand open at my command and the Gods themselves have been known to ask for my advice."

For all the strangeness of the encounter, Davey is becoming increasingly annoyed. The blue coated man seems to delight in teasing him and he is painfully aware that valuable time is passing away.

"I don't care who you are," Davey says fiercely. "Just as long as you can help me free Ruby Gilbert from the jail and get us safely away to the coast."

"Ah! So you've fallen for a rascally lass?" Perian winks. "I approve wholeheartedly."

"She's no criminal and I haven't . . . " Davey flushes.

"It is always the same." Perian shrugs. Davey opens his mouth to speak but the man holds up his hand to silence him. "Just let me see if I understand you rightly, Master Tachard." Perian's manner is quite business-like all of a sudden." You are requiring my help in the rescuing of a damsel from the prison house and the making of safe passage?"

Davey nods.

"That I can do, have no doubt, but what will you give me in return?"

"Take anything you like."

Perian raises an eyebrow.

"That is a very rash thing to say." A sardonic smile flashes across the Faery's face. "I may do just that."

"There's nothing valuable here, apart from my books," says Davey." I have two silver crowns under the mattress."

Perian glances about the room disdainfully and gives a dismissive wave of his hand.

"Even if you were as rich as a king, you would have nothing to offer me in the way of material things." Perian holds Davey's gaze, his eyes showing a glint of steel. "I trade in other currencies," he says. "I would take a promise, freely given, as payment for my assistance"

"Whatever you wish."

"You are bold enough," smiles Perian. "I'll wager that you will either die young and foolish or become a great man. It is hard to tell which of those it will be."

Chapter 26.

They leave the village in silence, hidden from sight in a twilight mist of Perian's making. Davey walks beside Perian, half in a dream. Despite the impossibility of it, there seems little doubt that the blue coated man is a Faery. Davey wonders how many of the old tales he has heard are true? Stories of Queen Mab and her enchanted palace below the earth, tales of mortal children carried away and never seen again. He recalls that most people in stories who have anything to with Faeries seem to lose their wits.

Davey realises, with a start, that they are already deep in the woods.
"Where are we going?"
"We are going to a place far from the haunts of men. A place where the veil between the worlds is thinner."
"Are we going to Faerie?"
"Not yet," replies Perian. "There will be time for that later. For now, we seek the passage to another realm."
"A passage to where?"
Perian flashes Davey an infuriating smile but makes no other reply. He leads Davey on, following paths that are little more than animal tracks.
"Even in the Twilight Land, my Queen has heard rumours of the exploits of Jack Shadow," Perian calls back over his shoulder. "It will amuse her to learn the truth." He laughs, the high music of it mixing with the bird song. "Queen Mab takes a great interest in the lives of mortals. I cannot understand it myself; for your little lives are so brief that one might as well

take an interest in the affairs of raindrops or of falling leaves."

"I thought that Queen Mab's servants came to our world in the shapes of animals?" says Davey,

Perian pauses and turns to Davey with a haughty look on his face.

"I am no mere serving sprite, master Tachard, I am Queen Mab's Messenger and one of her own race, the Immortal Sidhe. I take whatever form I choose."

Perian's face shimmers. In the space of a heartbeat, Davey sees a fox, an otter, a falcon and a stag. He sees a laughing child, a beautiful woman and an old man, all of them with the same unsettling eyes. Davey blinks and there stands Perian, grinning impudently.

Davey has many more questions but his tongue is numb with wonder.

At last, they come to a place where the brambles grow thick and impassable. Perian reaches out his hand and the briars part, the thorny stems sliding aside to make a dim, green tunnel through the wall of undergrowth. Perian leads Davey along the rustling passage into a circle of ancient oak trees. The wide trunks are cracked and rotten but the trees stand tall and strong, their topmost branches meeting high above their heads to make a leafy canopy. In the centre of the ring of trees is an open space where two tall, mossy stones stand. Beneath the moss there are shapes carved into the stones, strange looping letters that resemble beasts and birds. The clearing is utterly silent and there is not a breath of wind to disturb the dust of a thousand summers.

"I can remember the day that these stones were carved," says Perian." That was long ago, by mortal reckoning, ages before the grandfathers of these trees had sprung from acorns. In those days the Waking World and the land of Faerie were closer, more like neighbouring countries than separate realms, and the Sidhe ruled over them both." He gazes about the glade with a faraway look in his eyes. "Many worlds meet here and the paths are still to be found, if you know how to look."

The Faery walks to the nearest of the stones and puts his hand on it. He runs his fingers along the spiralling patterns and speaks softly in his own language. Davey cannot catch the meaning of the words but the sounds of them make his ears ring strangely.

The air between the stones darkens and a shape rises up, forming itself into the dim outline of a standing figure.

"Come from your rest, shade, and return for a space to the land of the sun and stars," says Perian.

"Who calls me?" asks the figure, in a voice as soft as shadows.

"Queen Mab's messenger calls you," says the Faery."It is by her power that I command you."

"What do you wish of me?"

"I have summoned you to aid one of your kin who lies in mortal danger. "

The shadow is more distinct now; a tall man wearing a black cloak and a wide brimmed hat. In the darkness below the brim two eyes glitter like shards of ice.

"And how shall you pay me?"

"You will be granted free passage to roam beneath the sky until I call you to Reavers Hill at tomorrow noon," says Perian.

The shadow sighs.

"I accept."

The dark figure steps from between the stones, becoming more solid as he does so. Davey sees a sword at the man's belt and a pair of pistols in a harness at his chest. The man stands for a moment, flexing his fingers and gazing down at his pale hands as if they are a source of great wonder to him. Then he raises his eyes toward Davey. The eyes are cold and deep and seem to hold the light of a different sky.

"You are the cause of my summoning," the man says.

"Yes," said Davey.

The shade smiles and his grey eyes twinkle.

"I am much obliged to you. I had never thought to walk in Bascome wood again, nor see the sunrise nor feel the wind. Nor did I think to meet any of my living kin again.

"I know who you are, David Tachard," says the shade." And I know the bargain that you have made to save the life of Ruby Gilbert. You are a brave fellow, I salute you." He sweeps off his hat and bows low to Davey, his long cloak swirling about him. He rises again and looks up through the leaves into the deepening twilight. "I have a scant few hours of freedom. I should like to ride upon the moors and look at the stars, for there are no stars in the realm where I dwell." He nods to Perian and touches the brim of his hat. "Until tomorrow."

The shade of Ned Sharpe steps away through the tunnel of briars and out into the forest.

In the wood he pauses, puts his fingers to his lips and gives a whistle. A sudden wind shakes the branches and tosses the bramble stems, whirling up a storm of dry leaves. When the leaves have settled a tall horse stands there, jet black from nose to tail. The beast tosses its head in greeting and the man steps nimbly up into the saddle. Without a backward glance, he turns his horse about and rides away into the forest, the horse's hoofbeats making no sound upon the earth.

"Why don't we go to the Court House at once?" asks Davey, when he is able to speak once again." If you can command the spirits of the dead then freeing Ruby from prison would be no task at all!"

"Patience," replies Perian."All will happen in its own time. Ned Sharpe must take his payment before he will aid us. And, as I have told you already, I am no magician. The power that I used was not my own, it was borrowed from Queen Mab." He smiles coldly at Davey." It must be paid for. "

"I have given you my word," says Davey.

Chapter 27.

Farmer Finch has taken off his boots and is stretching his aching bones out to the fire when there comes a sudden clamour of shrieking horses from the barn. He gets wearily to his feet, steps to the kitchen door and throws it open. At the gate of the yard something moves - a lithe blur of grey leaping the fence. Without bothering to put his boots back on, Sam Finch grabs up his shotgun and runs out into the moonlight.

  In the stable yard he finds his guard dog, Cob, crouching at the very back of his kennel, snarling and trembling with fear. It takes a lot to frighten Sam Finch but the sight of Cob so terrified sends a shiver down his spine. Checking that his rifle is properly loaded, he makes his way to the barn. The horses have calmed down but he can still hear them moving about nervously inside. Taking a deep breath he pushes open the door with his foot and raises his gun. "If there's anyone in there then you best come out slowly, " he shouts." I've got a gun."
There is no one there but the horses, pacing their stalls and tossing their heads.

   Finch lights a lantern and takes a turn about the barn. A quick circle of the farmhouse and yard shows nothing suspicious, until he glances up at the side of the house. The window of the little bedroom on the second floor is wide open, the curtain billowing in the breeze.

"I locked the door and closed the window tight," says Mrs Finch, as she and her husband run to Lucy's room. "The poor lass was terrified that the Squire would come for her."

The door is still locked but when they open it there is no sign of Lucy Cotton. The bedcovers are tumbled on the floor and the washstand by the window has been knocked over, breaking the water jug.

"Someone's kidnapped her! " cries Mrs Finch.

Sam Finch steps up to the window. The leaded glass is broken and the panels are bowed outwards.

"This window's been broken from the inside," says Sam." She must have jumped and run for it."

"Somethin' must have scared her rotten to make her do that. "

"What's this?" Sam squats by the shards of the broken jug. There are tracks in the spilled water that look like the paw prints of a large dog.

In the flower bed below the window, Sam Finch finds more animal tracks, but no sign of any human footprints. From the thorns of the climbing rose, half way up the wall, he plucks a tuft of silvery grey fur.

*   *   *   *   *

At the edge of the wood, a grey shape runs. The dream of the waking world is fading and Lucy is her night-self once more - a creature shaped by sorcery.

Long ago, when the Witch Wolves were made, Queen Mab chose the fiercest warriors to become her servants - bloodthirsty men with savage souls. The Squire had meant to make Lucy Cotton his servant and shape her in the image of Mab's Wolves but she has become something else; the spells have worked their transformation upon Lucy's body but they cannot bend her spirit nor bind her to the Squire's will.

By day, the wolf sleeps in the blood of Lucy Cotton, but when the sun sets, the wolf wakes and Lucy is lost until morning.

Silvergrey in the moonlight, she runs, leaping fallen trees, bounding through streams and shadows towards the high moor. She runs for the joy of it - to feel the wind in her fur and the earth leaping away beneath her paws. Long ago and far away, she was a frail and frightened girl. Now she is freedom. She is strength. She is swiftness.

As she gains the moor edge, she halts. The valley lies below her, the river a ribbon of silver between the trees. She lifts her head and howls. Nameless, wild and lonely, she sings her joy and sorrow to the moon.

Chapter 28.

Ruby's trial passes in a waking dream. She stands silent before the court, which consists of the Squire and a collection of dusty wigged old men so decrepit that they might have been dug up especially for the occasion. She does not answer the questions that they put to her nor even turn her eyes to look at them when they speak. There is no doubting where the power lies and no doubting the outcome of the charade. She hears the cracked voice calling out the verdict but it seems to her as if they are talking about someone else and she lets them lead her back to the cell without a word. It is dark in the jail after the brightness of the court room but she knows that she will not have to endure it for long.

The next day dawns grey and oppressive. The leaden sky has threatened rain all morning but none has come. At the top of Reavers hill, under the watchful eye of a troop of soldiers, carpenters have been at work since dawn, raising a gallows platform of roughly cut boards.

Long before noon, the crowd begins to gather at the crossroads. There has not been a hanging on Reavers hill for many years and rumours that the infamous Jack Shadow is a thirteen year old girl has spread across the county. Curious people have come from as far afield as Penzance and Exeter to witness the spectacle. There are pie sellers and a man with a cask of ale on a cart, who should by rights be doing a roaring trade, but few people are buying anything. A beggar with a violin sets up a tune but the gut scraper stops after he has played only a few bars. The music sounds wrong here; Reavers hill is a grim place, even in summer, and the gathering crowd huddle together in tight groups, speaking in hushed whispers.

When the soldiers are sighted coming up the road from Bascome, a cry goes up and everyone cranes their necks to get a good look at the figure standing in the back of the cart.

Ruby is dressed in a white shroud, with her hands tied behind her back. Her face is as pale as her gown, with a dark bruise on her cheek from the blow that Captain Ransome dealt her two nights before. She stares straight ahead, her face set and determined, while the soldiers in the wagon gaze nervously out over the crowd, holding tightly to their rifles.

The assembled throng watch in silence as the cart draws level with the gallows and Ruby is led up onto the platform. One jeering voice is raised but the call trails off as the man realises that he is alone. All about the scaffold the soldiers stand in close groups, watchful for any sign of trouble.

Ruby has never seen so many people gathered together in one place before. It seem strange that they should all have come to see her die. Some faces she recognises but most of them are strangers. She searches the crowd for those faces she most wants to see - those that she dreads seeing. Neither Seth nor Davey are there but she catches sight of John Summer, standing a little apart, at the back of the crowd. Their eyes meet for a moment and she reads the grief in his face.

She has let everyone down and she has been a fool. At least it will all be over soon. Her only comfort is that Davey, Tom and Seth have escaped. There has been no word of them and Ruby knows that the Squire would have been unable to resist taunting her with news of their capture. With any luck they are on their way to France by now.

Ruby looks out over the sea of silent faces. So many staring eyes. She is surprised to see some with tears. Others are expectant, drinking in the spectacle, waiting to see if she will break down or show Gallowsfoot Courage to the last. There will doubtless be a few wagers riding on that and she has decided not to disappoint them.

"Take a good jump at it," the jailer told her, as she was taken from the cell. "It'll be merciful swift then." Ruby has heard enough lurid tales of hangings to know that he is right; if she jumps then she will most likely snap her neck quickly and cleanly; a much better end than a slow, choking strangulation.

Ruby feels a firm hand at her elbow and the black hooded hangman leads her forward to the rope. At the sight of the noose, Ruby's courage almost fails her. She closes her eyes and takes a deep breath and the hangman, sensing her fear, pauses for a moment to allow her to collect herself. When Ruby opens her eyes again, her face is calm. She turns to look at the Squire, standing at the back of the gallows platform.

The Squire came to her at dawn and gave her one last chance to save herself. Ruby refused to

acknowledge his presence but now she looks him full in eye and curses him:
"You will rot in hell, Squire Colby. For an eternity of eternities may you be damned."
The Squire gazes back coldly. He makes an impatient gesture of his hand and Ruby is led toward the rope.

Ruby's senses are suddenly crystal clear. Beyond the lowering slopes of the heather clad hills she can see the ocean and the hazy line of the horizon. She catches the smell of freshly sawn wood and the faint taste of salt on the wind. She wonders what it will be like to die and realises that she is not afraid of what might come next. She feels only a deep sadness; for all its hardship, her life has been a wondrous thing and she wishes for more of it.

The hush of the crowd is a palpable thing, silencing the world. The birds have stopped singing and even the clouds seem to have halted in their rolling courses to watch. The crowd holds its breath as Ruby sets her foot upon the lowest rung of the gallows ladder.

The stragglers at the back of the crowd are the first to notice the horseman. No one marked his approach, but there he sits, tall and silent, swathed in a black cloak and hat, gazing toward the distant scaffold.

As the rider walks his night black mount forward the people step back without a word. The face beneath the wide brimmed hat is hidden in shadow but two eyes can be seen glittering there. One by one, the watchers turn away from the gallows to gaze up at the tall rider. He comes steadily on, parting the crowd like a slow reaper moving through a field of corn, the hooves of his horse making no sound.The sunlight seems to dim, as if dusk were falling, though it is only just past noon.

The Captain of the troopers steps forward and motions to his soldiers to raise their guns.

"Stand down man!" calls the Captain. "We are on the King's business here. Stand down I say, or I must order my men to shoot."

The rider pauses and turns toward the sound of the Captain's voice. Then he tips back his head and laughs. The rider's laugh sends a chill through the bones of all those that hear it.

"It is a merciful long time since any musket ball could trouble me," says the rider. His voice rings strangely, like a cry carried on the wind from far off across the moors.

There are gasps of fear from those close enough to see the rider's face. He is pale and handsome, with dark hair down to his collar. His cheeks are shadowed with stubble and a deep, crescent shaped scar runs from the left side of the mouth down to the tip of his chin. The rider's eyes are the grey of a storm over the ocean.

"It's Ned Sharpe," comes a cry from the crowd and a woman gives a stifled moan of terror. The onlookers fall back but they do not turn and run; the mesmeric will of the tall rider holds them fast and they have no choice but to look on in horrified wonder.

"That was my name once," the rider says in his soft, windblown voice. " I once rode these hills and I remember this place." His voice swells with anger. "I remember this place well!" The rider turns to the captain. "And I remember someone very much like you." The Captain opens his eyes wide and the colour drains from his face. The rider gives a contemptuous shrug and turns away.

"For God's sake!" Shouts the Squire. "Do your duty and shoot him down!"

The Squire's voice shakes the nearby soldiers from their trance. Several of them raise their rifles and they let fly a volley of lead. The noise of the shots sounds strangely muffled and the smoke from the gun barrels hangs like mist in the still air. The tall rider and his horse stand quite motionless.

"You are a fine one to speak of God," the rider says, turning his gaze toward the Squire. He walks his horse on until he stands beside the scaffold. He leans forward in the saddle and gazes into the Squire's eyes. "I know you, Nathaniel Colby," he says, "I know you and your kind very well." The rider spits on the boards at the Squire's feet. "You cannot hide your true name from me, nor can you cheat your fate forever."

It has been a long time since Squire Colby has been afraid but an unreasoning terror rises in him then. He wants nothing more than to turn and run but the highwayman's eyes hold him and he cannot move a finger.

"If it were up to me then you would be the one hanging here today," says the rider softly. "But it is not in my power to choose these things. The time and manner of your end are decreed by some other. Here, though, is a taste of what shall come."

The rider reaches out a gloved hand and, as the fingertips pass though his ribs, Squire Colby feels an icy darkness brush at his heart. He gasps, sinks to his knees, and falls forward to lie still on the rough planks. The rider straightens in the saddle and turns to the hangman.
"I have no quarrel with you," he says, fixing the hangman with his grey eyes. "You are simply a messenger. But I will thank you to release my kin and let her go free."
The hooded man lets go of Ruby's arm and falls back, trembling with terror.
"Come with me now," says the man on the black horse.

   Ruby has watched the rider's approach in a sort of trance. It is all so strange that she is not sure if she is alive still, or dead and dreaming some strange shadow dream? She looks back to see the noose hanging above her head, unused. She looks down at the Squire, lying at her feet on the boards.
"Come, cousin," says the rider. "Let me cut your bonds."
Ruby obeys the windblown voice and steps forward.
  The rider takes a dagger from his cloak and deftly cuts the ropes at Ruby's wrists. Then he takes her hand and sets her down on the ground before the scaffold.
"They are waiting for you, brave cousin. They are over by the fallen house. Be swift - I cannot remain much longer, the gates of the world are closing once more."

Ruby looks up at the rider. His pale, handsome face is impassive but there is a twinkle of humour in his grey eyes. He leans down and whispers into her ear and she feels the chill of his breath on her cheek.
"Those that have gone before are not gone. Our love does not fade, we carry it with us, always. Go now. May your life be long."
Ruby steps through the crowd and the people stand about her, still and silent as sleepwalkers. Their eyes are all turned to the dark rider and she does not think that they see her there at all.

  In the lee of the ruined farmhouse, just below the hilltop, two more horsemen wait. One she does not recognise. He sits, without a saddle, upon a slender dappled grey horse with a silvery mane and feathery white fetlocks. He wears a blue coat and his eyes twinkle with wild mischief. The other rider is Davey, mounted on Dervish. His face is pale but his smile, when he catches sight of Ruby, is warm. He jumps down from the saddle, takes off his cloak and throws it about her shoulders. He lifts her up in front of him and they ride away from Reavers hill.

  As they canter up over the moor top, Ruby hears the blue coated man laughing. It is a troubling sort of laugh, but she does not mind it; the world seems so altered that she does not think she will mind anything ever again. She sinks back into Davey's arms and feels the rocking gait of the horse moving below them.

Chapter 29.

They ride by paths visible only to Perian's eye, through dim hollows and forgotten glades, by stream banks lost in mist and meadows deep with wildflowers. They pass through sharp scented pinewoods where the air hums with bees and past herds of deer drowsing in forests of oak and honeysuckle. They move among a cloud of meadow larks and amidst the calling of crows, they pass through sun and through rain and they never once see any sign of human people.

At last, at the edge of a glade where a single grey stone rises up like a giant's finger, Perian calls a halt. The sun is sinking behind the trees and the clouds are alight with copper and gold. The blue coated man leaps nimbly down from his horse and turns to them. "You will find your companions a little way off," Perian says, nodding away to the East." I have fulfilled my part of the bargain. Do not forget your pledge, David Tachard." He fixes Davey with his fathomless eyes. "It will most certainly not forget you."

The little man gives a bow and turns on his heel. The dappled grey horse stands looking at them for a moment with a thoughtful air, before giving a little whinny and following Perian into the dusky forest.

Ruby has ridden all the way from Reavers Hill in a trance of wonder but now she feels suddenly wide awake.

"Who was that strange fellow, Davey? And what did he mean about a promise?"
"His name is Perian," says Davey. "Don't pay too much attention to what he says; he speaks in riddles most of the time."

In a wooded hollow overlooking the sea, they find Seth and Tom waiting for them. Ketch Avery is there too, hunched over a brushwood fire, stirring a pot of stew. He turns to them as they step from the trees and gives Ruby a friendly nod. Tom jumps up, a stricken look on his face.
"Ruby?" he asks in a whisper." Is that you?"
"Of course it is. Don't you recognise me?"
"But, are you . . .?"
Ruby looks down to that she is still dressed in her hanging shroud. Pale in the moonlight, with her feet bare, she is an unearthly sight.
"No ghost would make such a racket," says Ketch Avery, with a wink to Ruby and Davey. "I heard you comin' half a mile off."
"I'm quite alive!" Ruby laughs, hugging Tom.
Seth Gilbert's face lights up at the sound of Ruby's voice.
"It's good to have you back with us, lass," he says.
Katy is asleep at Seth's side, wrapped up in a cloak by the fire. As Ruby catches the scent of rabbit stew she realises just how hungry she is. She has had nothing to eat for the last two days.

Once she has eaten, Ruby is full of questions.

"Where are we going now?" she asks, wiping the wooden bowl clean with her fingers.

"Ketch has found us passage on a ship to Gravesend," says Seth."From there we will go to London. My sister Hannah will give us lodging until we have found our feet."

"London is a good place to hide yourselves," nods Ketch Avery." You'll be as hard to find there as a needle in a bottle of hay. But I'd watch out for the folks there. It's a city full of thieves by all accounts."

"I'd rather remain here, among honest folk," says Ruby, grinning at the smuggler. "But I suppose we can't stay in Cornwall."

Ruby looks over at the horses. Molly stands tethered next to Dervish and two of Ketch Avery's ponies.

"They came to the den on Pike's moor," says Seth."Dervish is a canny beast."

"Was there no sign of Caliban?"

Ruby's father shakes his head.

"He'll have gone back to his master," says Ketch.

"Back to the Manor?" Ruby doubted that somehow.

"Back to his true master - Old Nick."

Caliban would most likely be running wild on the moors. No doubt he would continue to be an unholy terror and sire a generation of fearsome wild horses.

  Ruby looks away to the West, to where Bascome lies hidden in the night. Is it right to leave like this? The Squire was humbled on Reaver's Hill but he is still alive and only she knows the truth about him - the evil that he is capable of. Ruby would not mind the risk involved in going back to put an end to Squire Colby but there are Seth, Tom and Katy to consider.

As much as she hates it, Ruby's revenge will have to wait. Once her family are safe in London, she will return and settle her score.

There are warm riding clothes for Ruby and two pistols on a shoulder strap. She puts aside the shroud, bundling it up and thrusting it deep into the hollow of an old oak tree. Davey mounts up on Dervish with Seth, while Tom rides one of Ketch Avery's ponies. Ruby rides on Molly, carrying Katy in front of her bundled in her cloak.

Katy wakes up as Tom hands her up onto Molly's back. She smiles at Ruby and turns to look about her. "Where's Lucy?" she asks, in a sleepy voice." I thought she was coming with us."
"She ran away from Finch's farm," says Tom."She was scared stiff, poor girl. She'll be half way back to Penzance by now."
"What about Jet and Bessie?"
"Farmer Finch will look after them. They'll be happy with him."
Katy nods, satisfied, and settles back into Ruby's arms.

They are the only passengers on the Lynster ferry. The Ferryman asks no questions, a handful of silver coins buying his silence.

The horses' hooves ring hollow on the floor of the flat bottomed boat and they snort at the unaccustomed sensation of the gently rocking deck. The ferryman signals to the man at the wheelhouse on the far side of the water and the winch horses take the strain, turning the heavy chain that pulls the boat across the sound.

They would have been happy with a fog to hide them but the night is calm and clear and as they cross the estuary. The water lies as still as a millpond, the reflected starlight burning almost as clearly in the dark ocean as it does in the deeps of the sky above. There is no sound but the soft plashing of the water on the prow of the boat and the distant clank of the chain winch on the far shore.

On the far side, they ride up along the coast to the headland, following poachers' paths through the woods to a glade above a little bay in the lee of Star Point where they meet a party of men with a train of mules. The men greet Ketch with a nod and together they descend the steep, shingly path to the beach.

Out in the sound a two masted ship is anchored. Ketch Avery uses a hooded lantern to signal to the crew of the brig and a longboat slips from ship's side. "Your ship is called the Swift," says Ketch. "Captain Lynot is the Master. He is a stern fellow, but a good Cornishman and you can trust him. He sails on both sides of the wind, if you get my drift, but as long as you keep to yourselves to yourselves, you'll get along with him fine."

Ruby says goodbye to Dervish and Molly, putting them in Ketch Avery's keeping, and once the cargo of barrels and bales have been carried ashore and lashed onto the backs of the waiting mules, the passengers wade out into the surf and climb aboard the longboat. Before they are halfway to the ship the beach is deserted once more.

Chapter 30.

Captain Lynot is a broad chested, grey-bearded man with a curt manner. He casts a shrewd eye over Ruby and her companions as they come aboard.
"I'll set you down at Gravesend, as I promised Mr. Avery," he says. "I know nothing of your business and you'll please me best by asking nothing of mine. If we chance to stop anywhere else along the way then that is no affair of yours." He nods to the cabin door in the middle of the deck. "There is a place for you in the hold, but you may remain above, if you wish, as long as you keep out of the way."
The Captain turns away and seems to pay them no more attention than the other items of cargo, which are stashed into every available inch of space.

Apart from Seth, none of the party has ever been on a sea voyage and now that they are safely aboard it begins to seem like an adventure. The anchor is hauled up and a gentle breeze rises, filling the sails. As the Swift slips out of the bay toward the open sea they stand together at the rail watching the dark coastline slipping away, listening to the water babbling under the wooden hull of the ship.

Ruby looks back toward Bascome valley, the hills and moors that she has known her whole life. Reaver's Hill rises above them all, the Bristol road a pale ribbon curving across its dark slopes. She thinks of the ruin of Gilbert's cottage and her secret glade in Fiddler's wood - what will happen to those places now? She thinks of her mother and all the others that they are leaving behind.

Something moves on the crest of the hill and she sees a rider there, silhouetted against the stars. The rider pauses and raises a hand and when Ruby blinks, the rider is gone.

Davey is looking out to sea and he has not seen. Ruby moves closer and takes his hand. Despite the sadness of leaving, it is good to be alive together under the stars and to feel the wind in her hair. It will be a long while before she will see Cornwall again but ahead of them lies the wide world, in all its danger and wonder, there to be explored.

The crew are too busy to pay them any attention, save for one old sailor who pauses in his work to stare at Davey. The right hand side of the sailor's face is disfigured by a deep scar that runs from his eyebrow down the corner of his mouth and he wears a patch over the place where his left eye should be. The man's good eye is as sharp as steel and the scar twists his lips into a permanent snarl. As the old sailor watches Davey a curious look of recognition comes over the man's face. Captain Lynot bellows an order and the old sailor turns away to haul at a rope, leaving Davey to wonder what the look might have meant.

As the wind becomes stronger the ship begins to roll on the swelling waves and the passengers make their way down to the hold. They find a snug place among the cargo and sit on bales of cloth and coils of rope. Tom lights a lantern and hangs it from a beam where it swings slowly back and forth.

Chapter 31.

By the cliffs at Star Point a tall needle of rock rises sheer a hundred feet from the waves. It is home only to gulls, who circle the rock constantly, calling out a harsh warning. The Giant's Spindle is the local name for the rock, after a tale about a Giant by the name of Castorax, who was tricked into trying to spin the swirling seafoam into silk. The rock is treacherously slippery, with few handholds, and no man has ever climbed it, though more than a few have tried. The wise ones gave up before they were a quarter of the way up, the foolish ones died, like the giant in the story.

On the very top of the pinnacle of rock is a flat place where thrift and seagrass have made a little lawn among the gull's nests. A man stands there, watching the Swift as she sails for the open sea. His coat is blue with silver buttons and he wears tall riding boots.
"Promises cannot be unmade," says Perian, bending down to pluck a flower from the rocks at his feet. "They have a way of returning to us, no matter how we might try to run from them."
Starlight flickers in Perian's eyes as he lifts the sea pink to his nose. He smiles, showing his sharp, pointed teeth, and then he is gone and where he stood there is only the night and a tiny flower falling, bobbing and twisting in the breeze, tumbling toward the ocean.

Chapter 32.

The first gust of wind hits the ship like a battering ram, ripping her sails and almost capsizing her. The deck pitches wildly and the sailors are thrown headlong, grasping at ropes to keep themselves from being flung overboard. Thunder booms and the stars are lost behind a rush of boiling clouds. The lantern is thrown from its hook to smash on the floor and the passengers in the hold are plunged into darkness. Katy screams and burrows into her father's arms.

Ruby is on her feet in an instant, stamping out the glowing lamp wick before it can set light to the spilled oil. As the ship rolls again she looses her footing and is flung sideways. Luckily for her it is Davey who breaks her fall.

"Ouch!" says Davey, as Ruby's elbow slams into his stomach.

"We've hit the rocks!" cries Tom, mistaking the crash of thunder for the breaking of the ship's hull. "We'll all be drowned!"

"Easy, lad," says Seth Gilbert. "It's only a storm. If we'd hit the rocks then we wouldn't be rolling this way."

The darkness makes no difference to Seth's blind eyes and he has ridden out his share of bad weather at sea. Holding Katy tightly with one arm, he winds the other arm around the wooden pillar at his side.

The cargo is sliding about as the ship pitches and finding something solid to hold onto is no easy thing. There is a crash as the rope holding the cargo of brandy barrels in place snaps and the barrels break free, thudding over the deck like giant feet dancing a demented jig.

Tom finds the pillar that his father is clinging to by bashing into it head first. A sudden explosion of blue stars swirl before his eyes as he slumps down over Seth's legs. Seth grabs Tom's coat and hauls him to safety.

Ruby and Davey are sent skidding together across the floor, rolling hard against the wall on the far side. Davey's groping fingers find a metal ring set into the wood and he holds onto it. He feels for Ruby's arm and guides her hand.

"Here!"

Ruby catches the ring just in time to save herself from being thrown back by the next roll of the deck. There is a splintering crash as one of the barrels breaks open and the hold is suddenly filled with the sickly stench of spilled brandy.

The waves rise higher, swamping the decks and pitching the ship about madly. The falling rain mixes with the flying seaspray until nothing is visible but churning water and torn patches of sky.

Captain Lynot has survived a hurricane off the Cape of Good Hope and a cyclone in the Azores, but the tempest that blows that night is more ferocious than anything he has ever encountered. A flash of lightning shows him how hopeless things are; the Swift had just cleared Star Point when the storm hit them and the wind is forcing them back toward the cliffs. He will have to turn the ship around at once to have any hope of avoiding the rocks at the base of the Giant's Spindle.

"Haul down the sails!" he roars. "Before the wind takes them!"

Once the sails are safe, Captain Lynot takes the helm and orders the first mate to rope him to the wheel. The rest of the crew take shelter where they can and pray for salvation.

Whether it is blind luck or the skill of her Captain that saves The Swift, it is impossible to tell. However it happens, when the ship regains the shelter of the bay, everyone aboard knows that they are lucky to be alive. Miraculously no-one has been lost, though a good deal of cargo has been swept overboard.

At the sound of the anchor being dropped, Ruby and Davey make their way up on deck to find the ship lying in the exactly same spot that she set out from. Breakers crash on the little beach below the point and a few last rags of cloud scud across the stars but, otherwise, the storm seems to have blown itself out as quickly as it came.

A group of sailors are busy repairing the torn sails, while the rest of the crew stand in a group by the forward mast. The savage looking sailor with the scar is deep in argument with Captain Lynot.

"Will you listen to me now, Captain?" says the old sailor. "My sunblind eye sees things that you cannot," He catches sight of Davey and raises an accusing finger. Every face turns." The boy has Mab's Mark on him," says the old man, lowering his voice. "The sea will not suffer us safe passage while he is aboard!"

Captain Lynot is a down to earth man and not much inclined to pay attention to the rantings of an old drunk like Bill Raven but it is clear that the rest of the crew are swayed by the old man's words. Sailors trust their lives to the whims of the ocean every time they set forth, which makes them the most superstitious bunch of fellows one could ever hope to meet. The Captain has half a mind to force the crew to set sail again at once but he does not care to test his authority. Besides, the way that the storm rose without warning from the clear sky has unsettled even him.

Captain Lynot turns to Davey.

"What do you say, Master Tachard?" he says, raising a bushy eyebrow."Are you a sorcerer?"

Before Davey can reply, Bill Raven steps through the crowd.

"If you've made a bargain with the Queen of Shadows then you had best keep it," he says, his dark eye fixed upon Davey. He turns to his shipmates. "We must set him ashore at once or we'll all go to the bottom."

"You are a fool to be afraid of a storm," says Ruby. "But perhaps you have some other reason to wish us ashore. How much did the troopers promise you to turn us in?"

Bill Raven hisses with fury and puts his hand to his knife.

"If you were a man, I'd gizzard you for that," he growls. "Bill Raven is no peacher." He turns back to Davey and pokes a calloused finger into his chest. "The lad knows full well what I mean. He is marked by a promise. Let him deny it!"

Davey stands silent.

"Davey?" asks Ruby.

"It's true," Davey says softly. "I have made a bargain with Queen Mab"

There is sharp intake of breath from Bill Raven.

"The boy will sink the ship if he stays on board, mark my words."

"Throw the Jonah overboard!" comes a shout from among the gathered sailors. There are mutters of agreement and several men step forward, ready to do the deed.

"The first of you to lay a hand on him will pay with his life," says Ruby, pulling a pistol from her cloak and leveling it at the advancing sailors. The men halt when they see that she means business.

"Easy lads," says Bill Raven, raising his hands for calm." There's no sense in drownding the lad. If Mab has set her mark on him then she'll hear of it, and she won't be best pleased." He flashes a malevolent grin at Davey. "From what I've heard of these things, the Faerie Queen will want him alive and breathing. We'd do best to set him ashore as soon as we can."

"You are not in command here, Mr.Raven," growls Captain Lynot. He and the old man exchange an ill tempered look and Bill steps back with a shrug. The Captain turns to Davey

"You have forced my hand," he says. "If you'll not deny this foolishness then I have no choice but put you ashore. I will carry the others to Gravesend, as I promised, but you must remain behind."

Davey nods.

"I'll not let him go alone," says Ruby.

Davey puts his hand on Ruby's arm.
"It's my bargain and I shall keep it. You must go with your father. There's no sense in both of us risking getting caught."
Ruby makes no reply but Davey can see from the fierce look in her eyes that she will not be argued with.

   There is no time for long goodbyes; now that the sea is navigable again Captain Lynot is eager to get away from the coast and the peril of patrolling Excise Men.
"We'll find you in London," Ruby promises, as she hugs Seth." We can be there in two weeks."

   When the moment comes to disembark, the crew eye Davey with murderous looks. They are all for making him swim the half mile to the shore and none of them will get into the longboat with him. It is only when Bill Raven takes the oars himself that they are able to get away.
"The sooner he's back on shore the better for us all," says the one eyed sailor as he climbs down into the skiff.
No one says a word as they row back to the shore and Ruby and Davey soon find themselves wading back through the ice cold surf to the beach below Star Point. They turn to stand, side by side on the shingle, shivering and watching the longboat pull away with Bill Raven at the oars.
   All too soon, the Swift has weighed anchor and unfurled her sails. Ruby can see Tom and her father

standing together at the rail and the pale blur of Katy's waving handkerchief, and then they are gone, lost from view as the ship turns into the wind. The sea remains calm and the sky stays clear as the Swift sails out into the open sea and around the headland.

"Mab's Mark and the bargain," says Ruby softly. "It has to do with Perian doesn't it?"

"It does."

"Then it's only right that I come with you. You saved me from the hangman with your pledge, so it is my bargain too."

Ruby wants to ask more, but there comes a scraping of boots on the shingle behind them and she spins about on her heel, a pistol in her hand.

"Whoa there!" says Ketch Avery. "We're not the Exise men."

Ketch and Will Avery took shelter in the wood above the cove when the storm came up and they waited there, watching the drama unfold, fearing that the Swift would be wrecked. When the ship returned they saw the longboat come ashore and came to investigate.

"Did you manage to fall out with Captain Lynot already?" asks Ketch with a grin.

"Something like that."

Ketch shakes his head and looks at them inquiringly.

"The others will be taken to Gravesend but we will have to take another way," Ruby says.

"You'll be wanting your horses back I suppose?" says the old smuggler, once it is clear that no more explanation is forthcoming.

"You're welcome to them. They are fine beasts but I'ב never sell them. The news of their taking will be all over Cornwall by now."
"We'll take them back gladly," says Ruby.
"You'd best be out of the county by sunrise."
"We'll be far away by then," says Davey.

Ruby and Davey mount up and, leaving the smugglers behind, head up the shingle path from the beach, Ruby riding Molly and Davey taking Dervish. As they crest the rise at the head of the cove Ruby turns to Davey.
"Where are we going?"
"To Smith's Den. Do you know the way?"
"Why do you want to go there? It's the other side of Bascome and the valley between will be crawling with soldiers - all of them looking for us!"
"I have no choice," says Davey. "You saw the storm. If I try to outrun my fate then things will only get worse. I have to fulfil my promise. But it's not too late for you; you can still ride to London to meet Seth and Tom."
"I'm not leaving you to go get lost on the moors."
They are exposed out on the cliff top, so Ruby leads them off at once, along a path between thorny hedges that run down into a sunken lane.
"Tell me about the promise that you made to Perian," says Ruby. "Why must we go to Smith's Den to fulfil it?"
Davey says nothing at first. He rides beside her in silence, gathering his thoughts. How can he begin to explain?

"I summoned Perian with a spell from the Squire's book . . ." As he speaks, Davey hears the strange words of the spell echo in his mind once more. The Keys of Queen Mab can unlock the power of the Faerie Queen's magic - the very magic that caused the sea to rise in anger and send them back to shore. Squire Colby has the book now. What awful things might he do with it?

He tells Ruby how Perian appeared and agreed to help in Ruby's rescue.
"But what was the bargain?" asks Ruby. "You still haven't told me that part."
"What Perian asked for in return for his help seemed like such a small thing. But now I am not so sure."

The blue coated Faerie had looked long and hard at Davey.
"In return for my help," he said."You must give me your promise."
"What do you want from me?"
"If I use the power of Mab's magic to rescue Ruby Gilbert then you must come before the sun has risen again, into the Twilight Land and present yourself to Queen Mab in her palace of shadows. She is fond of poets."
"How would I get there?" asked Davey.
Perian narrowed his eyes and smiled slyly.
"You will find the way," he said." The nearest path lies through the cave called Smiths Den. You know it, I am sure. Once you set your feet upon the path to Faerie, the doors of the nine worlds will open at your touch and no enchantment may hinder your coming

but, make no mistake, if you try to outrun your pact, then all the powers of the earth and sky will rise against you." Perian paused. He held Davey's gaze. "Once made, the promise is binding. Do you agree?"
Davey nodded.
"You must speak your pledge out loud so that the world may hear it."
"In return for your aid, I agree to present myself to Queen Mab before the sun has risen."
It had taken Davey only a moment to say the words but, once he had spoken, he felt the world change. The sunlight seemed to thicken and a stillness fell about them. The room had the same appearance as before but it was not the same room - it was as if they had stepped into a dream of waking, strange and vivid. There was a sudden depth to Perian's eyes that dizzied him and Davey sensed a current moving through the fabric of the world, as if a great, silent tide were carrying all that he understood away forever. From far off, came a snatch of music, the same eerie song that had followed him from Truro market. The music and the sensation were there for a moment and then they were gone.
"The bargain is made," said Perian."Let us go to the woods and summon the help that you need."

Davey shakes himself free of the memory and turns back to Ruby.
"I have promised to go to Queen Mab and read her my poems. I had hoped to outrun my pledge but there is no hope for it. I must go into Faerie," he says in a whisper. "Now do you see why I must go alone?"

"I'd like to see you try," says Ruby.

Chapter 33.

Ruby leads them by lanes and forest paths, keeping always out of sight and well away from farms or houses.

At the edge of the woods, they halt. Over the fields ahead lies the main road, rising up to Reavers hill on their right and falling away to Bascome on the left. There are hedges to either side of the road and beyond that the woods begin again. There is a gate in the hedge, not far off, but between them and the gate is a wide stretch of open ground.
"The path to Scarcrag and Smith's Den starts in the wood on the other side," says Ruby
They will have to cross the fields, in full view of Reavers hill. On the hilltop the outline of the gallows platform stands out starkly against the stars.
"Is there no other way?" asks Davey, tearing his gaze away from the gallows to scan the sky. He remembers keenly how the Squire's ghost hawk found them two nights earlier.
"We might circle through the forest behind the village, but that would take hours."
There is nothing else for it. They dismount and lead their horses by the reins, walking beside Molly and Dervish, stepping in the horse's long moon shadows, so that to a distant watcher they might appear like two riderless horses slowly plodding across an empty field.

It is a nerve-wracking walk, in full view of the hill top, but they see no sign of life save for inquisitive bats, who flutter so close about them that they feel the soft swish of air on their faces as they pass. They feel horribly exposed all the way and by the time Ruby and Davey reach the hedge, both of their hearts are thumping.

They have just reached the gate and Ruby is reaching to open it when they hear the rattle of cartwheels on the hill. A moment later comes the sound of horses coming up the hill from the direction of Bascome. There is no time to retreat to the safety of the wood, so Ruby and Davey pull the horses close to the hedge and hold on tightly to their bridles.

The drumming hooves draw closer, slowing to a trot, and the cart on the hill slows too. Through a gap in the hedge Ruby glimpses the red of soldiers' coats. "Halt!" commands the captain of the troopers.

The cart comes to a stop on the other side of the hedge from Ruby and Davey. Molly remains calm but Dervish senses the nearness of the soldiers' horses and snorts. She struggles in Davey's grasp and tosses her head. Ruby steps up to the chestnut mare and puts a gentle hand on her nose. She calms under Ruby's touch, her ears fall flat and she drops her head.

"Have you passed anyone on the road?" asks the Captain of the troopers.

"Only the mail coach," replies the cart driver.

"My men will search your wagon."

"Do what you will," the man replies. "You'll find no highwaymen hidden there."

"What do you know of highwaymen?" demands the captain.

"Only what I heard from the coachman. He told me that Jack Shadow had shot Squire Colby through the heart and ridden away from the gallows at the head of a troop of ghost riders."

"Squire Colby is as alive as you are," comes a new voice, hard and cold. "As for Jack Shadow and the Gilbert gang, they are being hunted down this very night by a hundred soldiers. They will hang soon enough, as will anyone who helps them."

Ruby knows the voice and she shivers at the sound of it.

"Only empty barrels on the wagon," calls a soldier. "Send this fool on his way, Captain," says the Squire."The fugitives must be on the road far ahead." With a rattle of wheels and a clatter of hooves, the cart sets off again and the soldiers gallop up toward Reavers hill.

When the sounds of cart and horses have faded, Ruby creeps to the gate. The road is clear and they lose no time in crossing to the far side.

To the left of the gate is a ruined house and the remains of a stone fenced cattle pen, to the right, is a hillside thick with thorn trees. Davey has just closed the gate behind them when Ruby catches her breath; a loping patch of darkness detaches itself from the shadows at the base of the nearest tree. The dark shape goes on four legs and its teeth glint in the moonlight.

Dervish rears back in panic and pulls free from Davey's grasp. She turns and bolts, running straight into the cattle fold. Molly tears herself free and follows after. The two horses are trapped between the high hedge and the stone walls of the pen and they back up against the hedge, shrieking, stamping and rolling their eyes in terror.

"Be still!" commands a harsh voice and the horses freeze.

Ruby and Davey turn to see Squire Colby step out from the shelter of the thorn trees.

The encounter with Ned Sharpe has left its mark upon Squire Colby, as has the repeated summoning of the Witch Wolves. He is pale and drawn, his eyes are sunk deep in the hollows of his cheeks and his hair has turned white from root to tip. The Elixir still works its magic but the illusion of youth is wearing thin. The Squire's voice is still powerful and his eyes glitter with malevolent triumph.

"The time has come for the final reckoning."

The command that stilled the horses has also bound Ruby's tongue and it lies in her mouth like a stone. Her feet are rooted to the spot and her hands are frozen at her sides. All seven of the Witch Wolves stand at the Squire's side, glaring down at them with slitted, yellow eyes.

"The soldiers may have missed the racket that your horses made as you hid behind the hedge but I did not," says Squire Colby. "If I had let the troopers arrest you then we would have had to endure the tedious business of another trial. The hangman failed in his duty the last time; I would prefer to do the job of killing you myself. I shall enjoy looking on as the Witch Wolves tear you to pieces and leave your bones for the crows."

The Squire speaks a word of command and the wolves leap forward, their lips snarling back over their cruel, white teeth. Moving as one, the wolf pack plunges down the hill like a dark tide, silent and deadly.

The movement of the wolves breaks the spell that holds Ruby and she turns toward the horses. There is little chance of outrunning the shadow beasts but they have to try - they might just make it into the saddle before the wolves catch them.

Davey makes no move to follow Ruby; instead, he steps forward into the path of the oncoming wolves. "No Davey!" Ruby shouts.

Davey flashes her a smile. It is a fey and dangerous look and it stops Ruby in her tracks. The wolves too, halt.

Ever since they came ashore after the storm, Davey has felt different. It is as if there is an invisible presence around him, a buoyancy in the air, as if he is a ship and a great wind fills his sails, propelling him onward. He recalls the words that Perian spoke when he had made his oath:

"Once you embark upon the path to Faerie, the doors of the nine worlds will open at the touch of your hand and no enchantment may hinder your coming."

Queen Mab's magic is all around Davey now and the wild fury of the storm thunders in his blood. He knows that the Squire's spells have no hold on him. He advances and the witch wolves fall back, retreating to crouch at their summoner's side.

"Your beasts cannot harm me," says Davey. "I am marked by a power greater than yours."

The Squire calls the word of command but the wolves do not heed him.

"By the hand that made you," says Davey."Return to the darkness where you dwell and do not come here again."

The wolves blink their slitted yellow eyes and slink silently away into the night.

The Squire gapes at Davey in wonder. Then, with a sneer, he draws a pistol from his coat.

"Where magic fails, brute force may succeed," he says, pointing the gun at Davey's chest. "You are still a mortal boy and I'll wager that a bullet will put an end to you easily enough."

A sudden shot rings out and the Squire's pistol jumps out of his hand and spins away into the darkness. Squire Colby stares for a moment at his empty hand. There is a deep gash across his palm and dark blood runs down to stain his white shirt cuff. He was so intent upon Davey that he had not noticed Ruby quietly drawing her own gun. When he looks up, he sees that Ruby had drawn a second pistol.

Silence falls.

Ruby grips the pistol handle tightly, the metal cold against her palm. The hammer is cocked and the gun is ready to fire. All she has to do is squeeze the trigger. At this range, she will not miss.

With Squire Colby dead, Ruby and Davey could return to Bascome, Seth might rebuild Gilberts Cottage and the Widow Marsh and all the others in the valley would be safe. Ruby has seen what lies beneath the Squire's mask and she knows him for the monster he truly is. Surely it would be a kindness to the world if she were to kill him?

Ruby wants more than anything to return to her old life but there is no going back; she is an outlaw, she has stared death in the face and walked free from the hangman's noose, she has seen the old tales come to life before her eyes and seen wonders and horrors in equal measure. Ruby hates Squire Colby with all her heart but still she cannot not pull the trigger. Or rather, she will not. Killing him will not bring her mother back or restore her father's sight. It will not undo the hurt that the Squire has caused.

"You deserve to die, many times over, for the things that you have done," says Ruby. "But I will not become a murderer for your sake."

"You do not have the courage to kill a man," says the Squire with a smile. "You are weak - "

"You know nothing!" snarls Ruby, her eyes flashing, her knuckles white about the pistol handle. "I will happily shoot you - if you wish it!" she lowers the gun so that it points at the Squire's knee and narrows her eyes. "Make no mistake. I will not miss my aim. I will lame you for life unless you take to your heels and run!"

There is such fire in Ruby's voice that the Squire takes an involuntary step backward. Davey's subduing of the Witch Wolves has shaken him to the core and there is an aura of reckless power about the pair of them that bewilders him.

"Run," hisses Ruby. "Run, before I change my mind and send you to hell!"

Squire Colby turns and stumbles away without a backward glance and is soon lost from sight among the trees.

"That was well done," says Davey.

"Perhaps," says Ruby, lowering the pistol."I may live to regret it."

"The Squire will get his just reward, soon enough."

"Sooner would be better." She turns to Davey. "How did you stop the wolves?"

Davey gives a shrug. His smile is gentle but the fey light still twinkles in his eyes.

"Now that I am on the path to Queen Mab's palace, I think that her power protects me."

"You took a great chance."

"It was the only one we had."

There comes the sound of hoofbeats on the road from Reavers hill.

"The troopers must have heard the pistol shot."

They take the horses by the reins and run to the edge of the wood. Molly and Dervish are nervous about entering the trees but Ruby and Davey have no fear of the Squire and his wolves now. They urge the skittish horses on and Ruby soon finds the track that they want. The sound of horses on the road is coming closer. Could Queen Mab's magic protect them from a whole troop of soldiers? They do not wish to find out the answer to that. They mount up and gallop for all they are worth, trusting to the surefootedness of their horses in the darkness of the wood.

As the sound of their hoofbeats fades, a silver grey wolf leaps down the hillside. She halts at the edge of the wood, sniffs the air, then plunges after them, silent as a shadow.

Chapter 34.

They ride through the woods and out onto heather clad hills, where Ruby finds a path winding between bogs and clumps of stunted trees. Unless you know the land as well asRuby does it is almost impossible to find your way here in the dark. If the troopers are still following then they have little chance of catching up with them before sunrise.

The stars fade from the Eastern horizon and the outline of Scarcrag rises above the edge of the moor like the tumbled ruins of a giant's castle. They ride on, until they crest the last hill and see Scarcrag directly ahead of them across the valley. Ruby points down to the shadowed cleft at the base of the tor: "Smith's Den is down there."

They sit side by side on their horses, resting before the last stretch of the ride. Steam rises from the horse's flanks, mixing with their breath and misting about them in the soft light.

"I wonder what it will be like in Faerie?" says Ruby.
"We will probably find that Smith's Den is just an empty cave," says Davey, wishing with all his heart that it might be so. "And that we dreamed all the things that happened to us these last few days."

Ruby says nothing. In the dimness of the moment before dawn, the world is a mutable place. The shapes of the land have not yet become fixed and one can so easily imagine the rocks and trees to be sleeping animals or the figures of men and women, waiting silently for the sun to rise.

Ruby is finding it hard to be certain just what is real any more. The warmth of the horse beneath her, the drumming of her heart, the cool of the air on her cheeks; these are all true things. She looks at Davey. He sits still on his horse, his eyes fixed on the shadows that hide Smith's Den. He looks solid enough, but there is a shimmer about him, as if he might dissolve with the dawn.

   A thread of gold flares on the horizon and a lark begins to sing high above, its wings catching the coming light so that it flashes like a tiny star. The valley below is still wrapped in darkness but it will only last a few moments now. Without a word, Ruby and Davey urge their horses down the hillside into the gathering light.

   As they near the base of the tor, a ragged figure rises from a rock beside the path. Davey recognises the hurdy gurdy player from Truro Market. His clothes have changed and in place of beggar's rags he wears a long coat of feathers that swirl about him as he walks. There are feathers from sparrow, kingfisher, crow and magpie, hawk, heron, swan and stormy petrel. All the birds of the forest and the sea are there. The feathered man turns the handle of his instrument as he comes, and the plaintive music lifts into the air, mixing strangely with the Lark's song
As the hurdy gurdy player draws closer, Ruby and Davey dismount.
"One of you is called by Queen Man," says the hurdy gurdy man, inclining his head toward Davey. "Your passage is paid with a promise." He turns to Ruby.

"The other comes of her own free will and must trade for her crossing. What will you give me?"

Ruby has no money. What about her pistols or her horse? As she looks into the hurdy gurdy man's faraway eyes she knows that none of these things will do. She remembers one of her father's stories:

"If you ever wish to return safe from Faerie, you must give up your most precious possession as you enter through the gate."

Ruby reaches up to unclasp the silver chain from her throat and puts the Kern into the man's outstretched hand. The amulet has not left her neck since the day that her mother put it there and it costs Ruby very dearly to give it.

"Currency of the heart," says the hurdy gurdy man. He lifts the Kern on its chain and the amulet catches in the rays of the rising sun, flashing like fire. Ruby gasps as the Kern changes; the time worn charm is bright and newly made, the lines of the horse are clear and gold sparkles in its mane. Silver letters run along the rim of the amulet and a green jewel flashes in the horse's eye.

"This was made in the Twilight, long ago," says the hurdy gurdy man. "And it remembers its true shape." He swings the Kern on its chain and catches it in his fist before placing it back on Ruby's palm. The vision has passed and the Kern is the same worn and dented thing that she has always known. "This key is yours, by right of inheritance. And it shall be yours until you choose to pass it on to its next keeper. As long as you wear it, the gates of Faerie will be open to you. It is a key to all the paths in the Nine Worlds. Trust its

power and you need never be lost." The feathered
man bows and turns away. "The Gate of the Dawn
will not remain open for long. We must hurry."
Ruby and Davey exchange a wondering look and
follow after him.

   The path narrows and they lead their horses on in
single file, Davey going first, following close behind
the man in the feathered cloak. The way winds down
into a deep gully, thick with mist. Cool droplets fall
on Ruby's face and the sound of their footfalls
becomes muffled. Shadows ripple in the dim air and
there comes the sound of distant music. The hurdy
gurdy man takes up the tune and begins to sing. At
first, the words make no sense but as they go deeper
into the mist Ruby finds that she can understand
them.

"Away from sleep, away from waking,
Through the door of the morning's breaking
Follow my song and take my hand
From sun and moon to the twilight land
Forget the earth, forget the sky
Follow me and forget to die!"

   Ruby and Davey are too entranced to think of
looking behind them and if the hurdy gurdy man
notices the silver-grey wolf padding after them into
the mist, he gives no sign.

   The shadows take shape, resolving into the branches
of trees with leaves as thin as gossamer. There were
no trees like these near Smith's Den the last time that
Ruby came to the cave. When she reaches out to

touch the ghostly branches her hand passes through them as if they are made of smoke.

The mist melts away and they step into a clearing. The strange trees rise tall about them, quite solid now, and the sky above is thick with flickering stars. There is no sign of Scarcrag or of Smith's Den.

Ruby rubs her eyes in disbelief but the vision remains.

In the centre of the clearing a host of men and women are waiting. They are dressed in robes made from feathers, fur or glimmering cloth that ripple like the scales of fish. Their beautiful faces are marked with a feral grace, as if they have, just a moment before, transformed from some animal shape into one very nearly human. Behind the Faerie host wait slender horses with silver harnesses. A group of handsome youths sit on the grass, playing soft music on a harps and flutes. They are clearly mortal and, though they smile as they play, there is a lost, empty look in their eyes. Beside the musicians stands Perian, with his unsettling, mocking smile.

For all the strangeness of the assembled company, there is only one face that draws Ruby and Davey's gaze; the tall woman at the head of the host, dressed in a white cloak and a dress the colour of new leaves. Her feet are bare and over her raven dark hair she wears a crown of wild flowers. Her skin is pale and her lips are the colour of freshly spilled blood. The Faerie Queen's eyes hold the blue of a summer sky, the fury of a storm, and light of the first star of evening. As she gazes upon Queen Mab's terrible beauty, Ruby feels dread clutching at her heart.

"David Tachard," says Queen Mab, in a voice both gentle and commanding. "You made a bargain with my emissary: In return for certain powers of enchantment, you promised to come and yield to my will."

"I am here at your command, Your Majesty," says Davey, bowing.

"Come away with us, word spinner, and leave the sorrows of the waking world behind."

Queen Mab beckons and Davey steps forward, his eyes wide with wonder.

"Davey - what are you doing?" stammers Ruby.

Davey makes no response and walks on as if she were not there.

"Why have you come here?" asks Queen Mab, turning her gaze on Ruby. "You were not summoned."

Ruby opens her mouth to speak but she can find no words. Like a mouse peeping up from the grass to meet the eye of a stooping eagle, Ruby freezes. There is deep magic in the Faerie Queen's eyes and not a hint of pity.

Queen Mab gives a cool, cruel smile and turns away. "Come with us now," she says, and Davey steps after her without a backward glance at Ruby.

Ruby shakes herself out of her trance, her anger making her brave again.

"I was the cause of the bargain that Davey made with you," she says. "He saved my life with his promise and I will not let you take him!"

Queen Mab looks back at Ruby, an amused smile on her face.

"I can see why you might love him. He is pleasing to look upon and clearly has a noble heart. But it would be such a shame to let him wither away. Your mortal lives are so brief." She turns to Davey. "Do you wish to come with me and live for ever in the Twilight Land or will you leave with this mortal girl and perish into dust?"

"I wish to spend all eternity making praise of your beauty," says Davey, his eyes never leaving Queen Mab's face.

"You don't mean that!" shouts Ruby, furious at the ease with which Mab has enslaved Davey - it has taken nothing more than a smile! Ruby takes hold of Davey's arm and pulls him back again. "Wake up, you dimwit! She has enchanted you - can't you see it?"

Davey turns and looks at Ruby but there is no sense of recognition in his eyes.

"Look at those fools!" says Ruby, pointing to the musicians gathered on the grass. "That's what will happen to you if you stay with her."

Davey shrugs Ruby off and turns back to Mab.

"I will go wherever you ask me, My Queen," he says.

"He has chosen," says Mab. "And the bargain cannot be unmade. You would do well to forget him."

"You tricked Davey into coming here and now you have bewitched him," says Ruby. "If he is to go away into Faerie then you must let him choose freely."

"We are already in Faerie, you fool!" says Mab, her eyes darkening. "You have come unasked into my realm and the penalty for that can be death, if I choose it."

They had only ridden a short way through the mist - how could they be in Faerie already? Ruby looks about her, at the flickering stars, the spectral trees and the silent figures in the glade. She is clearly not in her own world any more.

"The lands of Faerie and the Waking World are much nearer than you might think," says Queen Mab coldly. "In those places where the veil is thin, they are separated by a single step." Ruby does her best to hold Mab's gaze but it is not easy. She remembers the terrible storm that Queen Mab called up as they tried to sail away. She cannot fight against magic like that. Davey is gone - her family too - and she will die here, alone in the glimmering wood. She lowers her eyes and takes a deep breath.

Queen Mab is powerful in ways that Ruby can hardly grasp but what could she do that is worse than a hangman's rope or the foul schemes of Squire Colby? Ruby has survived these, and more, so why be afraid now? She lifts her eyes again and glares back up at Queen Mab. She trembles as she does so, but she does not feel the same unreasoning terror as before.

"Your Majesty," she says. "If bargains are the way that things are done here in Faerie, then I will make one of my own."

"I do not bargain with mortals!" replies Mab, narrowing her eyes in fury.

"You made a bargain with Davey."

Utter silence falls in the glade. It is a very long time since anyone has dared to speak so boldly to Queen Mab and all eyes are turned upon the mortal girl who stands, fragile and defiant, before the rage of the Faerie Queen.

Queen Mab's gaze falls upon the Kern. She frowns and reaches down to take it in her hand. All at once, the amulet is whole again, as it was in the hand of the hurdy gurdy player. The smooth gold glitters and the gem in the horse's eye flashes like a green flame.
"Where did you get this?" asks Queen Mab, her voice suddenly soft."I thought that it was lost, long ago."
"I was given it by my mother and she had it from her mother before her. It's been in my family for as long as anyone knows."
Mab looks intently at Ruby and smiles.
"You are very like him; foolish, bold and filled with that fleeting fire that makes you mortals so endlessly fascinating."
"Who do you mean?" asked Ruby."Who am I like?"
"He made a wager with me once." Mab smiles. "But he died long ago." Queen Mab looks away, her eyes lost in memory. In the silence Ruby feels her fate balanced on a knife edge.
"What would you wager?" asks Queen Mab at last.
"I will promise to take on any challenge that you might set me, in exchange for Davey's safe return to the waking world."
Queen Mab nods.
"For the sake of your ancestor, Wayland Smith, who made the key that you wear about your neck, I will make a pact with you." She turns to the Faerie host gathered behind her. "Bring me my crown," she commands.

A tall Faerie, dressed in a black robe, brings forward a silver crown set with flashing gems and holds it out for Ruby to see. The crown is carved with leaves, birds and animals and there are six large diamonds around the edge. The stones are the size of hen's eggs and clear as water. In the dimness of the Twilight Land they shine like stars. But the beauty of the crown is spoiled by an empty setting in its centre, a gaping hole dark as the eye of a skull.

"Long ago, the seventh star was stolen from my crown," says Queen Mab. "I have sought for it throughout the Nine Worlds but it has been veiled by charms that even I cannot undo. All that I know is that it lies somewhere in the Waking World. Bring me my lost diamond and David Tachard shall be released from his promise. If you fail then your own life shall be forfeit." Queen Mab fixes Ruby with her pitiless gaze. "Do you accept?"

"I accept."

"Then we shall meet a year from now, on Midsummer's Eve," says the Faerie Queen. She lifts her pale hand and Ruby feels herself falling, tumbling away through mist filled with flickering stars and swirling leaves. She hears distant laughter and a snatch of wild music, then silence. She falls on into the darkness and knows no more.

Chapter 35.

Ruby is woken by the wind. She is stiff and weary and her mind is a blur. She rolls over, puts an arm over her face and tries to will herself back to sleep but the ground she lies on is hard and the insistent wind reaches its icy fingers down her neck and sets her shivering. As her senses return, one by one, she hears the moaning of the wind and her nostrils are filled with the scent of damp and decay.

She opens her eyes to find herself lying in a dim place, half buried in a deep drift of fallen leaves. When she turns to look toward the light, she sees that she is in a cave. Trees grow close to either side of the entrance, their branches silhouetted against the blue sky.

Where is she? She was riding on the moors with Davey and they got lost. They must have taken shelter here.

Ruby gets to her knees and looks around. Molly and Dervish are standing nearby, huddled together with their heads down, their breath misting up before them in the cold air. There is no sign of Davey. She looks up again at the cave mouth. There is something familiar about the shapes of the branches. It takes her a moment to recognise the place; she is inside the cave at Smith's Den.

Where is Davey? Ruby's mind is still befuddled by sleep. They had been riding to Smith's Den last night and then . . ? She feels cold dread creeping over her.

Where has Davey gone?

She stands up, wraps her cloak about her, and walks stiffly to the cave mouth. What she sees there makes her gasp. She blinks and shakes her head but nothing changes.

Winter has come to the moors and snow lies over the land, deep and unbroken, smoothing the sharp edges of the crags, filling every gully and river bed. It was Midsummer when she rode into the valley with Davey.

Is she dreaming?

The bitter cold brings her memories rushing back like a blow; Davey went away with Queen Mab and Ruby is alone. She feels suddenly faint and reaches out to steady herself on a nearby branch. The Holly leaves cut deep into her hand, drawing a bead of blood from the ball of her thumb. She winces and draws her hand back. The gnarled old tree is heavy with thorny leaves and scarlet berries. On the other side of the cave, an equally ancient oak tree stands, leafless and white with frost.

The pain in Ruby's thumb tells her that she is not dreaming. She reaches into her cloak for the Kern and the familiar touch of it brings back the last pieces of her memory and she recalls the bargain that she made with Queen Mab.

Time moves differently in Faerie, all the tales agree on that. It seemed only moments to Ruby but how long has passed here while she was away? Queen Mab told her to meet again at Midsummer. What if Mab has tricked her? What if a hundred years have passed and everyone she knows is dead?

She lifts the hood of her cloak and a glittering thing falls to the snowy ground. She bends to pick it up. It is a leaf from one of the faerie trees. It must have caught in her hood as she fell. The leaf is as thin as gossamer and made from pure gold. The leaves had not seemed golden when she stood in the Twilight Land with Davey but things change as they pass through the gate between the worlds. Ruby has lost half a year in the blink of an eye, why should a faerie leaf not turn to gold?

Ruby stands at the mouth of the cave with the leaf clasped in her hand, hardly feeling the tears that fall and freeze on her cheeks. The winterbound moor gives no clue as to the passing of time. It is an ageless, secretive landscape that speaks only of desolation and loneliness.

At long last, Ruby's instinct for survival takes over and she turns to stumble down into the cave toward Molly and Dervish. She pushes herself down into the warm, musky space between the horses. She feels her legs give way and the two animals lean together, taking her weight and holding her. She lets the heat of their bodies warm her and loses herself in the soft thunder of their twin hearts, ringing like hoofbeats in her ears.

To find Queen Mab's lost jewel in the maze of the wide world - how should she even begin? Ruby feels for the Kern again. She remembers her father's stories and marvels that Wayland Smith really is her ancestor. The Kern is far more than a good luck charm. The hurdy gurdy man called it a key:

"It is a key to all the paths. Trust its power and you will never be lost."

Her newfound knowledge of the Kern's magic gives Ruby hope. She steps out from between the horses, pulls her cloak tight about her and takes hold of Dervish's reins. The wind is bitterly cold outside the cave mouth but the sky is clear and full of light. Ruby mounts up. Dervish gives a snort and a toss of her head, stamping at the ground and sending up a cloud of sparkling ice crystals.

"Don't worry about the snow," says Ruby, patting the mare's neck. "We'll find our way."

There are deep drifts on the windward slopes but Ruby can see the way out of the valley clearly enough. She turns to check that Molly is following and they set off.

They go carefully up the icy hillside and at the top they halt to look down at the land ahead. Under the clear blue dome of Heaven the moors below her are savagely beautiful. The sea is a grey shimmer in the distance and Reaver's hill glitters in the sunlight. A faint smudge of smoke shows the place where Bascome village lies behind a fold in the hills. Life goes on. The air is clean and cold and it is good to be on Dervish's back, riding together over the roof of the world. Davey is far away but he is not lost yet. They have vanquished the Witch Wolves and Ruby's family are safe. She has survived the hangman's noose and returned from the Twilight Land with her wits intact. Anything is possible!

The story of Ruby and Davey's adventures continues in the second instalment of The Gates of Faerie.
Coming soon from Deep Dark Forest.

If you have enjoyed this book then please consider leaving a review wherever you bought it. Good reviews help to sell books and the more books I sell, the more time I will be able to spend writing new ones!

Sign up to my mailing list to hear about the latest publications. You will also get a key to the Secret Glade, where you will find exclusive stories and other great stuff to download for free.
Go to **www.deepdarkforest.net** and click on the links.

You can follow me on:
Twitter @AJMwriter
Facebook@dreamsfromtheforest

I am always happy to get feedback from readers. You can email me at -
deepdarkforest@icloud.com

www.deepdarkforest.net

Acknowledgements:

Thank you to my wonderful wife, Sally, for inspiring me every day and for keeping Mondays sacred so that I could find time to write, despite the million other things that we have to do with our lives. Thank you to Elaine Miller for proof reading and for being my Mum. Thank you to Tina Betts, Rebecca Hill and Sarah Lilly for reading the manuscript at various stages of its life and giving helpful feedback.
Thank you to Roisin and Finn for letting me read the first draft of the story to them by the fireside, long ago.

Printed in Great Britain
by Amazon